Y0-BDE-490

NOTHING HAPPENED

NOTHING HAPPENED

EBBA HASLUND

TRANSLATED BY BARBARA WILSON

The Seal Press

Copyright © 1948 by Ebba Haslund
Copyright English translation © 1987 by Barbara Wilson
Copyright Introduction © 1987 by Barbara Wilson
Original title in Norwegian, *Det hendte ingenting*.

All rights reserved. No part of this book may be reproduced in any form,
except for brief reviews, without the written permission of the publishers.

This book was published with the help of the Norwegian Cultural
Council. The translator would also like to extend her appreciation to Ebba
Haslund and to the Norwegian Foreign Ministry for making possible a
stay in Oslo to work on the translation.

The cover illustration is a painting by Sigrid Hjertén, a Swedish artist
(1885-1948). "Den röda blusen" is reproduced with the permission of
Bildförlaget Öppna Ögon, Sweden.

Cover design by Deborah Brown
Text design by Barbara Wilson
Composition by Irish Setter
Printed on acid-free paper

Published by The Seal Press
            PO Box 13
            Seattle WA 98111

Library of Congress Cataloging-in-Publication Data
Haslund, Ebba, 1917–
    Nothing Happened
    Translation of: Det hendte ingenting.
    I. Title
PT8950.H337H413 1987   839.8'2374   87-4420
ISBN 0-931188-48-2
ISBN 0-931188-47-4 (pbk.)

10 9 8 7 6 5 4 3 2 1

Printed in the United States of America

INTRODUCTION

When *Nothing Happened* was first published in 1948 in Norway, it was almost completely ignored by the critics. Its author, Ebba Haslund, was thirty-one at the time; she had previously published a well-received collection of stories describing life under the German Occupation and a novel about a group of young girls, which had been labeled a juvenile book and not worth serious attention. *Nothing Happened*, the story of three young women students exploring friendship and love at the University of Oslo in the spring of 1939, met a similar fate. Dismissing the book was perhaps a way of dismissing its feminist and lesbian subject matter; one of the few critics to seriously review the book was horrified by its glorification of a "perverse" relationship.

Like many women's novels before it, *Nothing Happened* soon disappeared from the bookstores. Fortunately its author did not disappear as well, but went on to become one of Norway's best known and best selling writers. Over the last forty years Ebba Haslund has published ten more novels, another collection of stories, four collections of essays and six children's books. A noted critic and radio commentator, known for her acerbic wit and feminist sympathies, Haslund also became the first woman chair of the influential Norwegian Writers' Union from 1971 to 1975.

Seventy years old this year, she continues to play an active role in her country's literary and cultural life.

But what of *Nothing Happened*?

Although Scandinavian literature has a vibrant tradition of feminist writing dating back to the nineteenth century (Camilla Collett and Amalie Skram in Norway; Victoria Benedictsson and Frederika Bremer in Sweden), there have been remarkably few lesbian novels ever published there. In a recent study of lesbian literature in Scandinavia, *In Remembrance of Passions Past (På sporet av den tapte lyst*, Aschehoug, 1986), Gerd Brantenberg and four other researchers found six Norwegian novels with lesbian love as a main theme, thirteen Swedish, thirteen Danish and one Finnish-Swedish novel. And most of them have appeared since the 1970s and 1980s.

Before *Nothing Happened* was published there had only been one Norwegian novel that explored lesbian issues. Fittingly titled *A Confusion of Feelings (Følelsers forvirring)*, this novel by Borghild Krane came out in 1937 and describes the difficulties two young women experience living as lesbians between the first and second world wars. To anyone familiar with lesbian literature from that period it will come as no surprise to say that the story has a plot based on shame and hopelessness and ends tragically.

Nothing Happened deals with shame and repression as well, or more accurately, the *consequences* of having to be ashamed of and to repress who one is. Its difference, and its originality, lies in the fact that it combines a feminist perspective with its lesbian theme. The three main women characters in the book, Gro, Bente, and the narrator, Edle, are all, in their separate ways, in revolt against the roles society expects them to play.

As one may guess from its title, *Nothing Happened* does not have a conventionally happy ending. Yet it is remarkably free of the doomed sensibility of many early lesbian novels. The narrator, Edle Hendriksen, comes through her struggle to understand what happened in the past not only with insight, but with a growing self-acceptance. Writing at a time when there was no support from a feminist or lesbian movement, Ebba Haslund still managed to create a woman character who finally finds the courage to be honest, who finally begins to see what it might mean to love herself and to love other women.

Nothing Happened was republished in Norway in 1981. This is its first appearance in English.

Barbara Wilson
Seattle, 1987

NOTHING HAPPENED

» *Part One* «

I

IT'S NOT BECAUSE this day was worse than any other. When you take them one by one all these empty days are liveable. But when you take them all together!

My cup has slowly filled with useless, dreary days.

I've come to the point where I can't take it any longer; can't be bothered is maybe more honest. When I think of worn-out housewives slaving sixteen and eighteen hours a day, I don't feel I have anything to complain about, sitting here in my modern apartment, with a full stomach, with no one but myself to consider. A housewife way up north would probably call this a life of leisure. Though god knows, when it comes down to it, god knows if emptiness isn't the heaviest burden. All I know is that I can't take it any longer. I'm too tired. That's all . . .

Liar! That's not how it is. That's not the reason. Oh, if you could just be honest for once! Write it down and say it aloud, just the way it is, instead of hiding your head like an ostrich. You should grab yourself by the neck, rub your face in it, the way you do with dogs that have made a mess. Look here, look at this. Look what you've done . . . Start on a small scale, with the trivial little straw that broke the camel's back today. Instead of flailing around with high-sounding phrases, write about the emptiness and loathing you felt when everything came together in one specific little event—the encounter with Kit on the street today.

She was pushing a baby carriage; it was the first thing I saw:

3

Kit with a baby carriage. I hadn't seen her for years, not since
. . . that time. But I knew she was married of course—happily
married they said—and that she had children.

Poor children, I've often thought, having Kit for a mother.
Kit! Shallow, false, evil. No, not evil, just so taken up with
herself that she tramples everything around her. I thought of
my own so-called mother and toyed with the fantasy that I'd
get Kit's daughter as a student one day. An ungainly, stoop-
shouldered young girl, like me at that age, a pale, spindly plant
that had grown up crooked in the shadow of its resplendent
mother. But I would understand her and give her the tender-
ness and warmth she was hungering for. And when the ugly
duckling had become a swan—then Kit would have her eyes
opened. Then she'd come to me, powerless, embittered: "You
have taken my child!"

Idiot! Don't you ever learn? Every time your ego is stung by
a new scratch you immediately put a pink band-aid over it.
And under the band-aid the infection spreads until the whole
brain is inflamed, full of suppurating wounds that can't abide
being touched and that are covered with pink band-aids.

What sort of band-aid will I stick over Kit and the baby
carriage? Or should I give up my band-aids for once? What if I
make a cut instead? Right down to the bone, so it stings and
bleeds? Isn't that how you clean out a wound?

All right. I met Kit today in the street. I was on my way to
school for my fourth class, having been home during the break
to get a pile of compositions. As usual I was walking quickly,
my eyes on the sidewalk, and suddenly there she was right in
front of me; she came right towards me with the baby carriage. It was too late to cut across the street, to turn my head
away and hurry past. She'd already seen me.

"Edle! Hello!" in that dry little voice I remembered so well.
The only thing to do was stop, squeeze out a smile, say something or other—I don't remember what—in order to hold her
at bay while I closed up. I've become adept at protecting myself over the years. I'm not as naked and thin-skinned as I was
in high school. My defense mechanism works faultlessly. In
the course of a few seconds I was inside my shell, immune to

pinpricks. Oddly enough, they didn't come. There wasn't a single one, when I think back. It was only that I was so dreading what she *might* say that it felt just as bad. For the shell isn't thick enough that I don't *feel* the pinpricks. All it does is hide the scratches so whoever is hurting me doesn't see where they've struck.

But now, going back over what she said, I don't actually find a hint of goading or an ulterior motive, whichever way I look at it.

"Imagine—you're a high school teacher!" (But without sarcasm, almost as if she were saying, *Imagine, it's raining today*.) "Well, time flies" (with an affected little sigh). "And I have three children. Isn't that *impressive?*"

That was what she wanted to tell me. She was so full of herself that she didn't have time to stick pins in other people.

Impressive, certainly. She looked like a young girl. Clear-eyed, smooth-skinned and thin as a rail. Small and snippy as ever, just more dignified, more of a married woman. Elegant—in a squirrel coat and a tiny hat with a veil and furbelows. She hadn't changed a bit. Could have easily been twenty rather than thirty.

I knew she was expecting admiration. How wonderful she was looking, how young and unchanged. And who could believe she had three children! I should have clapped my hands together and said, "My goodness," and "You're amazing, Kit!" But I said nothing, even though I could have said it honestly. But not to say something was a small resistance against standing there tall and gawky in an ulster and muddy shoes next to her high-heeled, jeweled elegance.

She rocked the carriage. "This is my youngest—she's sleeping now—but you *must* take a peek at her—she's such a *sweetie pie*."

Sweetie pie! How like Kit. The sticky chatter. Cute and candy sweet when she thought it became her. Otherwise sharp enough at repartee.

I smiled coldly. Thought to myself that so far I was doing all right. The next moment the blow fell. Like a punch to the solar plexus. So unexpected, so—how can I explain it?

She bent over the carriage and pushed the quilt to one side, as carefully as when you lift away the tissue paper from a bouquet of lovely, fragile flowers. I stood there with my cold smile.

And then it happened. Not the baby; it was a completely ordinary baby, plump and pink-cheeked. I've never been particularly interested in infants, and only looked fleetingly at this one. It was *her* I looked at, *her* face as she looked at the child.

I'd expected something else. A self-satisfied expression of ownership, gloating—see what I've got and you haven't—the way she used to show off her newest acquisition at school. I was prepared for it. But she looked at the baby, tenderly, longingly, as if she wanted to hold it close to her, but couldn't, and had to content herself with just looking. I assume that's how mothers smile to their children when they're happy and love them. It was *not put on*. Not Kit Westman in the role of happy mother, acted out for a select audience consisting of poor Miss Henriksen. It was real. I can swear to it. That's what made it painful. It didn't have anything to do with me at all. She'd forgotten me and was smiling at the baby. A very normal mother smiling at her child. And that mother was Kit!

I don't know how I got away from there. I probably looked at my watch and said I had to run, that I had a class at school. I must have looked grotesque, galloping down the street with my ulster flying out around me and the bag with the compositions knocking against my legs. I held it by the handle as I ran. Kit must have wondered. She probably snickered, standing there on the sidewalk, and perhaps she burst out, as she used to in school, "Edle, how funny you are." She would have had good reason. Running like an idiot down the street! While the whole time the thought hammered inside me that the last time I'd parted from Kit I'd also run away. And my mind struggled blindly for protection against the memory of that time. Something was trampling me—not Kit—something larger and greater—indifferent feet were trampling over me. And something was pushing its way up, wanting to get into the daylight, something that threatened to burst open the old bandaged surface. I struggled against it, struggled with all my

6

strength to keep it down.

I succeeded. I'm sure I was myself at school today. Controlled, aloof. No one could notice any difference. But I knew it was only a matter of hours, minutes before I had to give in. Emptiness, the horrible emptiness I've fought with for years, now gapes at me from every side, and I have nothing, nothing to fill it with.

When I came home, I gave up. I lay for hours on the sofa, freezing and shivering, while a line of verse rattled in my brain:

"O Herr, gib jedem seinem eigen Tod
das Sterben, das aus jedem Leben geht."*

I've never had my own life. I've led an existence like millions of others, the existence that circumstance has provided for me. The days have passed as if in a fog; not one of these monotonous overcast days have I managed to make my own. I don't have the ability to break out and strike a new path through all the obstacles.

But what if I put an end to it all? Now, tonight. Of my own free will. At least then I would be choosing and willing the last act myself.

---

* "Oh Lord, give to each his own death
The dying that extinguishes each life."

II

Pᴇᴏᴘʟᴇ ᴅᴏɴ'ᴛ ᴅᴏ ᴛʜɪɴɢs like that—people like me don't, anyway. Definitely not. Sitting in the sober light of day, it makes me blush to read over last night's bombastic gush. I can't help being reminded of a parody of Racine I saw once. Grandiloquence and suicide. Ugh! Someone like me, at home with the trivial, has to watch herself so as not to aim for the tragic. She won't reach it, she'll only turn into a clown. But it shows how much it must have hurt, that meeting with Kit, when even I, a serious, ordinary person, had to think of something so drastic in order to bandage a wound.

Of course I knew I would never do it. Instead, I went to the movies and saw a spy film and then came right home and slept like a log (after just two pills) until morning. Coffee's brushed away the fogginess of sleep. I sit here in the dreary October light, uncomfortably clear-headed, reflecting on how unsuccessful I am and will be. That I can't even achieve my own death.

Outside, the Sunday street is quiet and dull. I can hear the faint, melancholy toiling of the church bells. They don't toll for me. I find it inconceivable that modern people, truly sensible, rational people, can bring themselves to believe in not only *one* god, but actually in *three*. Not to mention all that drivel about the Lamb and the Blood and the communion hocus-pocus. If you're going to believe that, you might as well do yourself in. It's Sunday today. Tomorrow's a holiday. And the cleaning woman isn't coming until Tuesday. I don't have a telephone and nobody ever comes here. You'd just have to take all the pills instead of two and slip more deeply into sleep, just like always. Only you wouldn't wake up. Painfully easy, rather like throwing out a pair of worn-out shoes. And all the same . . . it would be so impossible for me. I could do it about as easily as I could undress in the middle of the street. . . .

"Everything that happens to one is intrinsically like one-self." Huxley's books were, in the years right after high school, my favorite reading. And that one sentence has burned itself into my mind, is something I steadily return to. "Everything that happens to one is intrinsically like oneself." A dry, boring person is doomed to live a dry, boring life. Everything that happens to that person is necessarily of no consequence. One is locked into one's own trivial self with no means of escape.

All the same, I honestly meant yesterday's outpourings. The desire to be truthful was there, instead of the usual flight into hatred and self-pity. That meeting with Kit—at least I honestly tried to see it as it was, to see that Kit was in no way a monster, living off other people's blood. Just a normal human being. A good mother. Possibly a good wife too. Why shouldn't she be? She's cheerful and sociable; she's young and pretty and she loves her children. She's created her own little world, warm and snug. While my world is empty. She's definitely deserved her life, just as I've deserved mine. Perhaps she's not happy at all! Yes, she is. I saw she was. She was like a cat sitting by the fire, purring contentedly with her claws hidden. She's gotten what she wanted. But that naturally comes from having in her the talent to take what she wants and to enjoy the good that comes her way. Kit understands how to make a soft cheerful nest for herself and to fill it with precious objects. And I'm no martyr. Far from it. Just an infertile person who can't get anything to grow.

That's how it is. But what if I were to turn the same objectiveness on everything that went on then? Bring it up into the light and *look* at it, really look—instead of shoving it down. Maybe it would seem different then. Maybe it would shrivel up, shrink down to something small and harmless, everything

9

that I've been brooding over. Maybe it's just fantasy and nonsense. Or maybe . . . One thing is certain, I can't take it any longer. It's not working anymore. I see that myself. I must have clarity, put things in their place—so they'll stop churning around and grinding me into pieces.

It's been eight years. Eight years. It could have been yesterday. And it could have been another life. It's probably because the war lies in between. Those five long years. When I think about it, that's all, in fact, that I have to say about the German Occupation: five long years. . . . Other people have struggled and suffered, have matured or debased themselves—millions are dead. I've become five years older. What happened to me happened before the war. After that I was so busy licking my scabbed-over wounds that I didn't notice anything else. Now I regret it bitterly. It was a great, unforgiveable sin—mainly towards myself. And now it's too late.

Right after the Liberation flighty little Mrs. Holt, the crafts teacher, said to me,

"Goodness, we were all so sure you were working underground." She sounded rather disappointed. "We really believed you were one of the leaders, with your brain. You're just the type—so calm and cool. I would have thought for sure. . . ."

"No, it probably wasn't so easy to make contact," she said later. Consolingly! The stupid woman. But of course she was right. I should have participated. A lonely, isolated person like me. Well-educated, intelligent. I had nothing to lose; I would have met all the conditions. As far as making contact, how bitingly true! I had no contact! I have no contact whatsoever! It's as if there's a shell, a wall around me. The wall that went up eight years ago.

My unfortunate nature again. This sick desire to dramatize, to make a great tragedy of a thoroughly trivial affair. That's not how you come to understand things objectively.

Therefore, nothing happened. Absolutely nothing. It was just me hoping, and believing and misunderstanding. Nothing of importance has ever happened to me—apart from

Father dying when I was four and Grandmother when I was eleven and Mama marrying Alfred. But Mama has never meant anything to me, has been nothing but a negative force because of everything she isn't. And Alfred is and was plus/minus zero.

I've managed to reach the age of thirty without having experienced anything of importance. I don't count my exams. Naturally it was satisfying to graduate at the top of my class and score highest in the final exams. But exams aren't real life, not what people generally reckon as "experience."

Let me nail it down firmly: in reality, nothing happened at the time. And my shell began to grow long before. I think it started one day many years ago when that lady passing by described me as "the most hideous little girl" she'd ever seen.

I must have been quite small, because it was before Alfred. Five, six years old perhaps. We were living at Grandmother's. I was playing alone outside; I was in the middle of a game of hopscotch on the sidewalk when she came by and said that. Not to me, but to the person with whom she was walking. I don't remember now if it was a man or a woman. But I remember her words and I can hear them to this very day, with that condescending smile in her voice, as if she were pointing out an amusing fish in the aquarium. I remember that I turned beet red and ducked my head so she couldn't see. I threw my charm bracelet any old way and hopped after it, without noticing where it landed. And when I decided they'd gotten far enough down the street, far enough away so they couldn't see me any longer, I cut and ran, through the gate and across the courtyard, up to Grandmother, and on the way I stumbled and scraped my knee on one of the steps. I still remember how glad I was to have *that* to cry over. And how long and how bitterly I cried.

There have been lots of incidents like that. They are the black flecks in the gray tweed. Bente had a suit like that during high school; the material was thick and light gray with large black flecks. It suited her, went well with her dark hair and tawny skin. I've never owned anything like it. I am too gray. Gray-minded and gray-skinned. From inside to outside—gray.

III

As far as I can see, there are two things that have had a decisive effect on my life, from childhood to the present day: my ugliness and my intelligence. The latter is by no means an asset—on the contrary. If I'd just been ugly, I would have lived a modest, wallflower existence. I would have been spared the pinpricks. Not only would I not have felt them, I wouldn't have received them either—at least, not so many or such poisonous ones. I would have lived the unnoticed, peaceful life of a wallflower. But right from the first day of elementary school my intelligence has thrust me in front of the footlights for general observation, for ridicule and derision.

An ugly woman is an anomaly, a monstrosity, for whom no one has any use. Her place is in the background, in the hidden corners, where she can make herself useful in a modest way. But she must not venture to front stage. That's presumptuous and offensive.

I'm so sick and tired of hypocrisy. "These days one's appearance means *nothing.*" Or the myth of the ugly girl who was so ugly she was actually pretty—whether that's explained by a figure that compensates for the irregular features or by so much charm that you forget to notice anything else. But how can an ugly woman, a really ugly woman—like me—ever get the opportunity to develop any personal charm?

It's possible I was born without charm. But even if I'd had a germinating seed of charm in me, it definitely would have shriveled up in this pinprick atmosphere. No charm in the world could survive that!

"You're so intelligent," and "You're so clever," and "You're so incredibly talented"—that's what they've said for years, but always with a sting of pity. As if all that talent and intelligence were really a meager compensation for my ugliness: the long, sharp nose, the broken-out forehead, the stringy, mousey hair. Poor Edle Henriksen, who's not very attractive!

I've always been tall and ungainly, with large hands and feet, flat-chested, gawky. My walk and posture go along with it. I trudge around with long steps and hang my head so as not to be seen. I know it's worse that way, that I should shove my shoulders back, straighten my skinny body and walk with head high and quick steps. But I can't. Not out in the street among people. I've *tried*, but I can't do it.

It's the same with colors. I *know* that gray and dark blue are the worst colors for me (after black, which makes me look like a vulture). But gray and dark blue are merciful colors that hide, that erase. They don't scream, "Get out of the way," like red and electric blue and purple.

"Why don't you buy yourself a bright red outfit?" Gro said once. "It'll put some color in your cheeks—brace you up."

And I, idiot that I am, went right out and did it. It was the spring when everything happened—or more correctly—when everything came to nothing. And I can still hear Kit's voice, "Edle! Is it you? God, how you scared me. I thought it was a fire engine!"

I gave away that suit. During the Occupation years I rather regretted it. It was almost new, after all, of excellent material; I could have dyed it dark blue. But at the time I thought only of getting rid of it.

Red isn't for me; it never has been. I've always been ugly: "the most hideous little girl." Later I became "Edle, who's not very attractive, poor thing." Now I'm Miss Henriksen. Or just Miss.

Oh, how I hate them, sitting there smirking and raising their hands. "Miss!" "Oh, Miss!" Hypocritically eager, pretending that they're burning with interest in history and geography, when the only things on their minds are clothes and boys.

Remarkably enough I've never had any difficulties with discipline. They sit still as mice during my classes. I think they're afraid of me. I know they are. I know their sensitive spots, and don't mind if I touch them. I've seen them duck their heads, red-faced, seen their stupid dolls' eyes fill with tears while a servile snickering comes from the desks around. But no one has ever dared snicker at *me*. They believe I'm immune from such childish scorn. They don't even try. They believe it's useless. And so long as they believe that, I'm secure, safe in my shell. But not as invulnerable as they believe. I too once had naked, defenseless skin, but it was flayed off me, strip by strip. And that won't happen again. No, that won't ever happen again.

"Everything that happens to one is intrinsically like oneself." Locked up for life inside myself. Well, better that than to be lulled by false hopes and expectations. There was a time when I thought I'd actually broken out. And since that time I've been grieving, bitter and spiteful, because I didn't act differently, handle it differently, *wasn't* different, so that things could have taken another course and I could have remained in paradise. Wouldn't it have been better to realize at once that the whole thing was an illusion? That it was the lights and shadows of other beings, more optimistic and colorful, that happened to fall on my path, and that I was only reflecting their glow? And that it was natural for the glow to vanish when our ways parted, leaving me just as poor and dreary as before. "Everything that happens to one . . ."

When I think of the others, those who have meant so much to me, I see the same logic in their lives.

Bente—my first real friend. My only one. For it was different with Gro. She was so independent, so free. Gro was for everyone, and not for anyone in particular. But Bente was always my friend. A strange, rough friendship. Bente who loved sports and excitement, who created trouble and rode straight through all the conventions at a breakneck gallop.

Bente with the defiant smile and strong, tanned, boyish fists that twisted and bent life to the way she wanted it. Proud, arrogant Bente—and boring Edle, who erased herself.

What did Bente see in me? I've often wondered. Perhaps she thought I was brave and unconventional, because I was so unfeminine, so completely different from the usual young girl. What's certain is that she invented for me many of the qualities she valued herself and that I've never possessed: courage, self-assurance, the ability to charge straight ahead without worrying what other people thought. That's how she wanted me. And perhaps that's how I was—with her along. It was as if she stirred me up, like military music. Everything was on a heroic scale with Bente. When I think about the rebellious young girl in high school, the black sheep of the class who lived in steady opposition to the school's authorities, and about the woman who left her nice husband and her good home in that small town to plunk herself down in my studio room to "get some breathing room," then I can't say I'm surprised by Bente's "illegal" activities during the war. Kit mentioned them yesterday. "Imagine Bente, it's so amazing. She's been a real Joan of Arc. Who would have thought it?" But Kit has always been blind to other people.

To me it seems completely natural that it was Bente who made such a contribution, natural that she transmitted secret radio signals to defy the Gestapo and ended up fleeing across the North Sea in an open boat. That she returned home after the Liberation in a lieutenant's uniform and was decorated for courage. Just as natural as that Kit is married to a merchant and has three children and that I am a "Miss" at a girls' school.

Hans Jørgen still lives in this city, writes a little for the newspapers, translates a book now and then, and receives a couple of lines of praise in book reviews for his cultivated and flowing prose. About the same as before. I see him in the street occasionally. Just last week he sat in front of me at the movies. It was the first time I'd seen him again close up. Strange that it wasn't more harrowing. I merely felt uncomfortable and slightly disappointed—the same as when you find an old toy you had as a child and are surprised at how small and faded it's gotten. Quite impartially I registered that his hair had grown thin and that his overcoat looked vaguely shabby. I already knew eight years ago that he would never amount to anything. Strange and unsettling to think that he was the cause of my heart's deepest wound. Like being run over by a bicycle. Or drowning in two feet of water. "Everything that happens to one . . ."

And Gro . . . That is a wound that can never be healed, Gro dead in Germany. She's *gone*. As soon as I close my eyes she's there, clear as day. She comes striding over the main square at the University, right to me, bare-headed, wearing big heavy high boots. The wind blows her trench coat out like a sail and ruffles her unruly dark blond hair. She's wearing a high-necked gray sweater that curves tightly over her breasts and a plaid pleated skirt. And her face—but I can't remember her face, and I have no photograph. It's terrible that I can't remember Gro's face. Just her mouth, that's all I remember, her wide smile.

Her eyes? Were they blue or brown? Closer to brown, I think, with flecks of gold. Her smile was in her eyes too. It was a broad face, that I remember. Broad forehead, wide jaw. Broad. And alive. Light and shadow rippled over it like the sun on a fresh windy April day.

Gro . . . it's inconceivable that you're gone—that you are no longer. And all the same, what is more natural than that you, who were life itself, had to fight life's battle against the powers of darkness? And than that you won. I know you won. They said that, your comrades. You were your glowing self to the end.

She died in a German concentration camp of tuberculosis. Gro, the picture of health, so strong and healthy. Gro, coughing, weakened, feverish? I try to imagine it. But all I see is tousled bangs and a wide, smiling mouth. Gro dying of T.B. It's easier to see her standing before the Gestapo, straight-backed, unafraid, full of defiance. But no, that doesn't fit. There was no defiance in Gro. Only that wide, restorative smile that accepted everything.

»Part Two«

I

IT WAS AN EVENING just past New Year's. I sat here at the desk
and read Ferrero's *Rome's Greatness and Decline*. I remember it
as if it were yesterday.

I had only been here a few months and living in a studio still
had a glow about it. As if some pressure had been removed. I
could breathe freely, could be myself. Joy in my new freedom
and independence went together with joy in my studies. I felt a
kinship with the Humanists waking from the Dark Ages, with
Erasmus and Ulrich von Hutten; full of the thirst for knowledge and the desire to investigate. "*O Jahrhundert, o Wissenshaf-
ten! Es ist eine Lust zu Leben! . . . Die Studien regen sich und die
Geister blühen auf!*"* . . . It felt something like that.

I opened up Ferrero the other day and read a couple of chap-
ters about Octavian and it was as if a breath of the old fresh joy
wafted up from the book's page, joy at reading and mastering
a subject, joy at being free and peaceful, leaving behind my
irritation with Mama, living my own life, independent of others—a joy that has long since dried up.

Mama and I weren't getting along anymore. To be sure, she
had become resigned, had finally given up the hope of making
a presentable daughter out of me. As far as that went, everything was fine. She'd stopped intervening in regard to my
clothes, my appearance, and my behavior. She had tried as far
as possible to ignore all that and to treat me like a casual fellow

---

*"Oh Century, oh Knowledge! It is a delight to be alive! Study stirs and
minds flourish."

passenger or hotel guest. Too much to ask of anyone, naturally, as long as we were under the same roof and I was still her
daughter. It *couldn't* work, in spite of our joint attempts. For
once we both pulled in the same direction. She let me go my
own way (which must have appeared mysterious to her), and I
repaid her by keeping out of sight as much as possible.

But, of course I couldn't totally disappear. I *was* there the
whole time, like an irritating foreign body, thin and sharp-
nosed, the ugly and peculiar daughter of the house. People felt
duty-bound to ask after me. "How is Edle?" "What's Edle
doing these days?" Or to be embarrassingly specific, "Where
is Edle tonight?" They were never able to answer, "Oh, she's
out dancing," or "She's at a party!" Instead it was always, "At
the library." "At the reading room." Or more correctly, "In
her own room." It was almost as embarrassing as having me
there in person, tall and gawky in the midst of a group of
elegant, sparkling guests. There was always a little lull in the
conversation when I came in. They made obvious efforts to
talk to me. And it didn't make it any easier for me when I saw
how hard it was for them. Oh, that forced, cheerful tone that
was supposed to hide the compassionate distaste in their voices! I suffered, and Mama suffered. All her hectic chatter about
university studies and intellectuals couldn't explain away the
one central thing, that "Mossa's daughter is unusually home-
ly, poor dear."

I can't say that I have any particular sympathy for Mama. I
am the only point of friction in her otherwise smooth and
comfortable life. And when you've brought a child into the
world, then you have to put up with it, however it looks and
acts. But for Alfred, who got me full-grown, I'm sorry. Poor
Alfred Bugge, how sad for a jovial, kindly and rich man, who
appreciates good food, pretty girls, Strauss waltzes and risqué
jokes to get a dry stick like me for a daughter. Alfred never
says anything. He would rather not hurt his wife's feelings.
But in his innermost heart he has certainly sighed for a fair-
haired little girl, who could entertain the guests and sit on his
lap and run up huge bills in the city's fashionable shops. At any
rate, it was a relief for all of us when I finally moved out on my
own.

I clearly remember that evening. Outside, the rain poured darkly against the window. The streets glistened black. There was no snow around New Year's that year. I had been at the library, had sat reading *Roman Emperors* under the weak lights; everyone there was sick with colds, coughing and hacking. They were mostly older—lecturers, fellows, here and there professors—the students hadn't yet returned from the holidays. Many seats had been empty, and an atmosphere of timelessness and unreality had suffused the reading room, that of scholarly research, the Humanities; muffled, padding steps.

The light from my green desk lamp now fell over the smooth pages of Ferrero. I turned the leaves, reading, sinking steadily deeper into the material. The mood pervaded the air around me, cozy and intimate.

The doorbell rang, short and impatient, once, twice, and finished with a piercing clang. The snug stillness was ripped apart. It didn't occur to me that it might be a pleasant interruption. It had to be something annoying. A message from Mama perhaps, an irritating encroachment on my hard-won peace.

I clomped out to the hallway, yanked the door open. And there stood Bente, soaking wet—water poured off her—in a white raincoat, red kerchief and shiny black tall boots. No gloves, no purse, no umbrella. Her hair was hidden under the kerchief, stiff and dark from the rain, and her face was bare and beautiful with droplets on the smooth, tawny skin. I can see it again, as it shone out of the rainy dark January evening: the straight Greek nose, the high cheekbones and partly open mouth, the upper lip slightly lifted over large white teeth—defiant and stubborn.

"Hello," she said. "I called your house and got your address. May I come in?"

I hurried to get her inside and stammered some unnecessary phrases about how nice, what fun. . . .

Bente nodded, smiled, stripped off her raincoat and kerchief, kicked her boots into a corner and padded inside in her socks.

In the center of the room she remained standing, looking around for a few moments while I waited anxiously.

"Wow, it's nice here," she finally said. "All by yourself and no one to share it with. A lot nicer here than in that pink maiden's bower you had at your family's. *I* think so anyway." She padded around a little. "Simple and nice. Exactly how I'd have it. A sofa and bookcases, a couple of good chairs and a huge messy desk. And not a single photograph. What a blessing!"

I smiled with relief. While I was still wondering what I should offer, suggest, do for her, she threw herself into a chair, stretched out a slender brown hand and pulled me down on the armrest.

"Don't make a fuss now, Edle. Can't we just sit and talk a little? Or maybe I'm disturbing you terribly?"

I assured her that she wasn't at all.

"Fine," said Bente. She dug around in her jacket pocket— she was wearing the old light gray suit with the black flecks that I remembered from high school—and pulled out a crumpled pack of cigarettes and offered it to me. I declined and she lit one, took a couple of deep drags and leaned back in the chair.

"I've moved into a fleabag hotel downtown. My suitcase is there. But I had to talk with someone. And it had to be you." (Her words exactly.) "You're basically the only friend I have. I've gotten so far away from the others in our class and, anyway, they'd just be shocked. You see," said Bente and leaned over to knock off the ash. "I've left, escaped from the whole damn mess."

"Oh," I said weakly.

"Yep," said Bente. "I couldn't take it. Not one more day. Maybe you know I have a marvelous husband named Sven Arnesen and live in Lillevik in a cute little house with a garden and have the world's nicest in-laws and . . ." she bent over and knocked the ash off again, a little unnecessarily, "a sweet little boy, seven months old. And now I've left the whole business, because I couldn't take it." She looked me directly in the face.

What was I supposed to say?

"Are you going to get divorced?" I tried and blushed. It sounded intrusive.

"I don't know," said Bente slowly, wrinkling her forehead. "Damned if I know. I suppose it may come to that. Sven will probably want to. Boy, but he'll be mad. The scandal, you know! I can just imagine how it will get around in Lillevik. 'Guess what—young Mrs. Arnesen has left her husband. And he's such a wonderful man! Oh my goodness!' I went off without leaving an address, just wrote a note, like in the novels, you know, about needing some breathing room, and so I was leaving. Period. Yours, Bente. He'll probably come rushing here tomorrow. Search all the hotels. Sven is so thorough. He's bound to find me. But damned if I'm going back." She got up and padded up and down the room.

"What have you thought about doing?" I asked, mostly to say something. Something disquieting, foreign had come into my peaceful room. I felt strangely elated and dizzy, as if I'd just inhaled strong cigarette smoke.

"I don't know," said Bente. "Damned if I know. What are you doing?"

I told her that I was in Humanities, that I had two minors and History as my major.

She nodded.

"I really should have taken Physical Education," she sighed. "And maybe English as a minor. Then I wouldn't be sitting here now with nothing to show for myself. But you know I got engaged right after graduation. I'll be damned if I know how it happened. It was the two of them together, Sven and my father! And I was just a kid. Yeah, I wanted it too. Both wanted and didn't want. You know how it is. But later . . . I decided to get out of it. I *had* decided. It's really true, Edle. I *wanted* a proper education and to stand on my own two feet and make something of myself. If Sven was against that, it was better we broke it off. I was totally set on that. And then suddenly my father died."

She stopped, overwhelmed.

". . . That turned everything upside down. It was so unexpected. He was only fifty-one. Standing there operating one day and lying there dead the next. Inconceivable . . . One day ruling with an iron hand, exerting his influence on everything.

The next day losing his grip . . . I felt like I was falling backwards, the way you do when you've been pulling on something with all your strength for a long time—without any particular hope of getting it loose and suddenly the whole thing snaps and there you are on your back with the handle in your fist, and there's no point in anything anymore."

She was silent again.

". . . There *was* no point in anything. No point in fighting back or showing you could amount to something. I was so tired and sad; I just dragged around. Like a homeless cat, with no place to go. Sven took charge and arranged everything, you know. My aunts thought he was wonderful. It was Sven this and Sven that. No one else needed to lift a finger, least of all me. He was so considerate and sensitive and understanding that I almost wilted from sheer respect. It makes you totally passive, like lying on a mattress that's far too soft; you just keep sinking down and can't manage to get up again. It was as if there were nothing to do but marry Sven. He talked me into it; I said yes, okay, all right."

I have a clear picture of Bente as she sat there that first evening, collapsed in the chair with her chin on her chest and her legs stretched out. I have only to close my eyes to see it before me, sharp and clear, as through the viewfinder in a camera. She's curling and uncurling her toes in the red socks and staring out from under knitted brows. The brown, boyish hands hang loosely over the arms of the chair and the cigarette dangles between her fingers, a thin stream of smoke trickling up through them.

I sat on the edge of a chair, tense, watchful. I didn't want to mess this up. I had to say the right thing, put on the right expression, be everything Bente expected. Not pedantic and narrow-minded, but liberated, understanding—trustworthy.

But intermittently, the thought came rippling warmly through me that Bente was sitting here in my studio, confiding all this to me. It had to be you! The same breathless expectancy you have in the theater just before the curtain goes up— that now it's beginning—finally! I don't know what I expected. A new existence—the fulfillment of all those hazy expectations springing from my new independence. I know now that this was the prelude to my strange leap out of character that spring—Bente's visit. The illusion that she needed me. Along with my first clumsy attempts to raise myself to her level—a level of activity where something was always happening.

Everything began that evening. Bente lit fresh cigarettes, smoked, stubbed them out, spilled ashes on the floor—and talked—talked without ceasing. She'd always had those sudden eruptions. I remembered them from high school. She could be silent as a clam for weeks on end, then suddenly explode on the most inconvenient occasions, when no one had time to listen.

There wasn't a thing she didn't tell me that evening, about her marriage, her in-laws—everything—cold and matter-of-fact, as if they were total strangers she was speaking of, and not her close relatives.

It was as if the room began to fill with people. You had to strain to follow along, to take in everything that was offered, higgledy-piggledy, and all at once. And the whole time I sat wishing, wishing fervently, that Bente really meant to break off with him, that she would be serious about it and settle down here. The thought of all the possibilities that would open up made me completely giddy. To be able to meet her often—perhaps daily. Bente as a companion, as a close friend! Someone who needed me, not just as a reference book and course or text advisor, but as a friend her own age, an equal!

Bente kept talking. About the pregnancy—the long months when she was going through it—getting clumsy and heavy—and Sven who was tender and protective and proud as of a first-rate breeder. About the birth itself, which was "horrible but terribly exciting."

Bente as a mother! It seemed unbelievable when you looked at her slapdash, boyish figure. I risked a question, vague, uncertain, about how it felt to have a child.

She wrinkled her forehead and answered slowly, "I think I'd love him better—I *do* love him, it's not that—only I don't enjoy little babies that much. But when he starts walking and

23

can talk and everything, and I can take him with me on walks and show him things and talk to him and *be* someone to him— it will be different. But I think I'd have been more taken up with him if he hadn't been the whole Arnesen family's baby— with Sven practically bursting with pride—and my mother-in-law talking so poetically about the 'joys of motherhood' and 'maternal feeling'—and me just standing there like an icicle, a little embarrassed, because I don't feel as splendid as whoever she's going on about. And when I'm passing by the crib and feel like touching him, straightening his comforter or something, then Sven shoots up out of nowhere or my mother-in-law does—she's in and out of our house the whole day— and one of them puts their arm around me and whispers 'little mama' or something like that . . . that drives me *crazy*. And when they talk about how sweet and delightful and cute as a bug, I get the urge to tear off all the lace the nanny has dressed him in and stick the child under my arm and get out!"

She took a violent drag from her cigarette.

"Yes, he has a nanny. They probably don't trust me to take care of him myself. I can almost hear my mother-in-law: 'You know, Bente is so *young*. And it's so *good* for her to get out a little and not be so tied down.' Get out a little, she says! In Lillevik! Sit around sipping tea and chatting about diapers and househelp and Mrs. Pedersen's trip to Oslo. Sure, it's wonderful having a nurse, naturally. And they *are* nice. And I *do* love the child. But he's not *mine*. Do you understand? And right now he's chaining me to the Arnesen family."

I remember I squirmed. Bente was so coarse, so recklessly frank. It was hard to know what to say.

"It was Christmas that spelled the end. Christmas in Lillevik. In the bosom of the family. Well, you can imagine it yourself. Christmas at the in-laws with a Christmas tree up to the ceiling and eveyone singing carols, hand in hand—starry-eyed expressions on their faces as if they were children again. And little Harald on his papa's arm—cute as a bug! And then, god help me, it was the same comedy over and over every single day the whole Christmas time. Them at our house—us at their house—aunts, uncles, brothers-in-law, sisters-in-law.

24

During the mornings it poured and there was no place to go! New Year's Day the whole bunch gathered at my parents-in-law's—for a change—and just as I was sitting there, fighting to keep the pork down, it struck me. My god, you can leave, you know. You don't *need* to be here. I became so happy that I was quite pleasant the rest of the evening. My mother-in-law and sisters-in-law looked at each other—meaningfully. But it didn't bother me a bit. It actually didn't feel so horrible anymore, knowing I could leave when I wanted. It offset all the sentimental drivel, just to know that. Maybe I could have held out a little longer. But the next morning my mother-in-law 'dropped by' and sat there for three hours talking about the joys of motherhood and 'little Bente who's motherless herself,' so nicely and tactfully that I was ready to throw up. So afterwards, while Sven took a nap after dinner—they do that in Lillevik—I packed my suitcase . . ."

I was no longer listening. I sat putting the finishing touches on something that I'd been wanting to say. A suggestion, unexpected and bold as Bente herself. Wanted it to sound nonchalant and buoyant. At last it slipped out.

"Can't you camp out here in the studio with me? I mean, until you figure out what to do?"

I blushed immediately, hearing how gauche it sounded. And the words *camp out*—I simply hadn't managed it. They sounded strange, like foreign words.

Bente looked up. Surprised. Glad as well. But by no means thunderstruck.

"That's damned nice of you. Do you really *mean* it? It would really be fantastic. But are you sure it's okay with you?"

I hurried to reassure her; I clucked and cackled like a scatter-brained hen. No trouble in the least. It would be a pleasure, it would be fun. . . .

Bente looked me full in the face and said, "You're a real pal, Edle."

Those words exactly.

II

It turned out the way I'd dreamed and hoped it would. With Bente there a new life began, refreshing, varied, strenuous—all at once. It was as if there were always a gust blowing through an open window. Not that Bente herself caused a fuss—she's the sort who can live out of a knapsack and thrive.

I remember a cousin, a niece of Alfred's actually, who stayed here overnight some years ago. She took hours to unpack and to arrange her things; there were underwear and toilet articles everyplace. The bathroom was cluttered with flacons, tubes, jars and used cotton balls. And after she was gone, a sweet heavy fragrance still hung in the air, tenaciously reminding me of her.

Bente had a folding cot she slept in and a chair to drape clothes over at night. Those she wasn't wearing lay in a suitcase under the bed. In the bathroom she had a glass with a toothbrush, a brush and comb, a large bathtowel and a bar of soap—brown tar soap—I can still smell that fresh, stinging scent. Bente even looked like an English schoolgirl, scrubbed, aseptic, in a red flannel robe and red slippers, chemically free of feminine charm and fragrance. She washed her hair herself, once a week, and brushed it with a hard brush. It always looked nice, dark and smooth, lying in a shiny coil around her head. She smoked countless cigarettes, but always kept the ashtrays emptied and aired the room thoroughly. "I can't stand it stinking like a bar," she said. It was only the first evening that she dropped ash on the floor.

No, Bente was no trouble. But it was exhausting all the same. I felt obliged to balance on the same tightrope she did, to be as devil-may-care and straightforward and self-confident. The air was thin and I strove every day to acclimatize myself.

She returned to the hotel that first night, but she was back here the next day with her suitcase. My mother loaned me the folding cot and extra bed linen; she thought it was so wonderful. "Imagine that, *you* having a friend to visit." And thus Bente was installed.

The University opened that day. It had gotten a couple of degrees colder; it was sleeting. Downtown the streets were muddy, filthy black, ugly. The cars spurted brown sludge and people staggered along dejectedly, as if to a funeral. And there we were in the foul slushy weather, getting the school catalog and clearing up Bente's student ID. It was a blue Humanities ID, with a small photo taken at high school graduation. Bente Moe Arnesen. She had to have Arnesen on it. That upset me.

I remember how cozy it felt to come home to warmth and light and to take off our soaking wet boots. We sat cross-legged on the sofa and drank piping hot tea and made plans for Bente. She decided to take Philosophy and Latin for spring semester and do the introductory courses in Phonetics and Linguistics at the same time. I hinted that it might be too much, doing three semesters worth of Latin in one semester along with everything else. I wanted to make it sound exciting and difficult. "That's true," was all she said. But I saw she was determined to manage it.

I had made up my mind to direct Bente into Humanities and to get her to cut Physical Education. There was no rush, for the time being at least, to make a decision, but it wouldn't hurt to start trying to persuade her. I told myself that a Humanities degree was the only right one for Bente. Still, I had to do it cautiously.

The whole time there seemed to be a secret tug of war between the unknown Sven Arnesen and me. I had immediately decided to get Bente out of his clutches. It was up to me to do it. Because Bente herself—I had an uncomfortable feeling that Bente was wavering—she wasn't as certain as she pretended.

It showed in the hectic way she threw herself into her studies, piled up classes on her schedule, far more than she could handle. It was obvious she needed a bulwark, something she could barricade herself behind when Sven came.

We both waited for Sven, waited tensely, while we pretended it was not at all important. After the first evening we no longer exchanged personal confidences. Lillevik wasn't mentioned. But the tenseness was just as strong; it quivered like a vibrating chord under our daily life.

I dreaded a scene. My hands could get wet and clammy just thinking about it, and I thought about it continually. What would he say about me? And how would Bente handle it? Would I have to play an active role or could I keep out? I was so afraid I'd do something stupid, something that would irritate her and bungle everything.

Every time I saw that defiant, arrogant smile of Bente's, I thought elatedly, *He'll never manage it.* But during the night, when I lay awake, listening to her even breathing, everything felt impossible. Sven would appear with the child in his arms, with all Lillevik behind him; he'd talk and talk until Bente shrugged her shoulders and went with him. In restless, troubled dreams I saw her wandering like a sleepwalker out of the room, back to Sven. And all my begging and pleading was useless. She just stared at me with wide-open eyes and walked past me without a word.

The first week was as long as a whole semester. We got up early and went to the University together. Bente had a Latin class at eight and I had to be there early to get a seat in the reading room. During the break at eleven-thirty we met for lunch in the student dining hall. We ate dinner out. Then we came home, drank coffee, read, chatted, and went to bed at a decent hour. I was used to staying up reading through the night and to making up for it by sleeping late some mornings. But Bente swore by a "normal daily rhythm." So I went to bed early too, and gave up reading in bed so the light wouldn't disturb her. I'm sure it was healthy. But at first I lay awake a lot.

All the same I wasn't tired; on the contrary, my spirits were high as never before. An undercurrent of excitement held me up; it shook up all that was ordinary and affected me like a powerful stimulant. That's how the first week was, charged with expectancy, no Sven in sight.

Bente worked hectically, going to three and four lectures in the morning, conjugating Latin, studying phonetics, psychology, the history of philosophy—all at once.

"Strange there's not a peep out of him," she said one evening, as if that were something we discussed every day.

This new tactic, which the mysterious Sven had devised, made me angry. I hated him for reacting differently than Bente had expected, for weakening her initial powerful resistance.

But I didn't say anything. I didn't want her to suspect how interested I was. She wouldn't stand for meddling. And if she noticed that I was trying to hold on to her, she'd break off, throw me over just as she'd thrown over Sven.

"Have you thought," I said lightly, "that if there's a divorce, you'll get the child? So far you haven't done anything so awful that they can call you an unreliable mother."

"I did leave though," said Bente uncertainly.

I explained that it took a lot for a mother to be denied the right to her child.

"Oh," said Bente. "But I can't take the boy away from Sven. That would be—dirty." She got up and took a few steps across the room. "I should write and ask him to arrange things financially," she said soberly. "I have a little from Father, and I could probably use it for my education. Anyway, I'll go through with all the exams at the end of this semester. Then we'll see. . . ."

She showed me the letter before she sent it. It was short and businesslike. She told him she was living with me and gave him my address. No explanations, no reasons. Just that she intended to take such and such exams at the University. "Hope everything is fine with you and the boy," she ended. "Yours, Bente."

A few more days went by. Bente chainsmoked every evening, conjugated Latin, almost never talked. And I hated that

Sven—hated him so my blood boiled, so I had to clench my teeth. I hated him that much. But I didn't say a word.

Precisely a week after the letter was sent came the answer. It lay on the floor under the letter drop when we came home for dinner—a rectangular, white envelope with large, flourishing writing, not small and cramped as I'd imagined.

Bente ripped it open and read the letter while standing out in the entry. Then she hung up her raincoat without a word and threw the letter and the envelope on the desk.

I remember she stood by the window with her back towards me, and I busied myself elaborately at the desk, tidying up notes, putting pencils in their right places. And the whole time the letter and ripped envelope lay there.

"Well?" I finally asked, when the silence began to thunder.

"Read it yourself," said Bente monotonously. "If you feel like it."

I didn't answer, kept straightening the pencils. I didn't want her thinking that I was interested in other people's letters, that I was dying to stick my nose in her business.

"Go ahead and read it," she said. "I don't mind. I can't be bothered to repeat the whole thing. It's much better if you read it."

She sounded friendlier and I understood that the sullen voice wasn't for me, but for Sven. He was the one she was angry with.

Awkwardly I took the letter; my eyes wandered to Bente standing at the window with her back towards me. Then I unfolded it and read:

"My darling little Bente:"

I couldn't help turning red. And I had the same embarrassed feeling the whole time I was reading. He hadn't written before because he'd wanted to think it over and not to write anything stupid or rash. There it was. I saw before me a series of letters, written in anger, in passion and bitterness, torn into pieces and begun again, an evolution of letters that had ended in this single, well thought out, irreproachable husband's letter.

He understood that she needed a change, that she needed to get away from Lillevik. He'd thought of suggesting it himself, but she'd beaten him to the punch! It would be good for them, for both of them, to be away from each other a while. The boy was in good hands, getting the kind of care he was used to— she already knew that. Otherwise she wouldn't have left. He'd already taken care of her financial situation. All she had to do was go to the bank. Not a word of indignation or mention of any sort of uproar. Just a few lines at the end. They went like this:

"Everyone here thinks you're wise in taking a little time off during this gloomy period of the year—and that they rather envy you your trip to the city. I would have liked to have taken a trip to the big city myself, but I have so confounded much to do. Enjoy yourself a lot and write when you feel like it. Say hello to your girlfriend. It's nice you can live with her and not have to stay in a pension. Hearty greetings and a kiss from your Sven."

I especially remember the capital "H" in "Hearty." It had a flourish all its own. I stood there with the letter in my hand and felt as if something had been punctured. I looked at the un-moving gray back in front of the window and thought, How *could* she have gone and tied herself to that man? She'll never get free.

"Have you noticed that it's snowing?" asked Bente. "That's fine, I can go skiing on Sunday. I haven't had skis on for two years."

But her voice was gray and flat. It drifted over me like a clammy, blanketing fog: no use, no use—might as well give up now as later.

III

SPARKLING WINTER-WHITE DAYS came along, days that cleared the clammy mists from my mind and filled me with a quietly shimmering joy. When we trudged down Drammensveien in the morning the streetcar tracks hummed and their wires crackled and sent off sparks; people's voices rang out. We bunched our hands up in our ulster pockets, talked quickly and a little breathlessly, as the air froze our throats. Perhaps it was Bente's purely primitive happiness at walking rapidly, stretching her muscles, feeling the sting of the cold that I found so contagious. There was something about those winter mornings, something high-spirited and glittering—they come back to me now. Once I too felt like that. How could I forget!

The Oslo basin steamed with frost as we tramped down through the middle of it. Only the cupola of the National Theatre rose up out of the thick fog bank. It was lit by the morning sun and glowed rosy pink by the time we parted at the University's main square.

Coming into the cheerful warmth of the reading room was another pleasure. You stretched, rubbed your hands, felt the frost lose its grip on your stiff fingers and toes. Each new person who came in brought with them a breath of crisp winter weather, red cheeks, bright eyes, a nose white with frostbite at its tip. People smiled and nodded, still a little out of breath. The eternal sniffling around the tables seemed less depressing. Everyone sniffled when they came into the warmth, because of the cold outdoors.

When all the seats were occupied and quiet sank over the reading room, we sat at our tables turning pages silently, sharing the cheerful coziness of being there together while the rime glittered on the trees outside. Suddenly a long beam of red-gold sunlight poured in over the opened books. "But when rosy-fingered Eos . . ." Every time I see that over-used little verse of Homer's, I feel a small frozen joy—a pale reflection of that time.

I had been lonely at the University. After Bente arrived and became such a necessary part of my daily life I understood *how* lonely I had been. Student life was in many ways different than I had imagined it. I got along well enough—in fact I got along remarkably well. I had my studies and they devoured me. It was a pleasure to be able to work independently, to really get into the material, to push on steadily without having an entire sluggish class like a ball and chain at the ankle. But I didn't find any friends. My attitude then was different from now. I wasn't closed up inside my shell, didn't have a negative or hostile view of the outside world. It was shyness and awkwardness for the most part. I hid myself away, afraid of seeming obtrusive, afraid of being clumsy, afraid of making a fool of myself. During high school the University seemed to me a kind of intellectual heaven, a paradise of culture and scholarship, a gathering place for the country's intellectual youth. I'd wished myself away from the chatter and frivolity of my girls' school, longed to take my rightful place in the coming new world, to find a spiritual home where I could take root. But it didn't turn out like that.

The University was old and decrepit, not venerable like the places of learning on the Continent and in England. Just plain old-fashioned. Filthy. With smoking, coke-burning stoves, peeling paint and an underground women's restroom reeking of urine from overflowing toilets. Yes, of course, the renovations of 1938, when Domus Media was furnished with new cloakrooms and reading rooms, had helped. Though undoubtedly the original building is still as antediluvian today as

33

ever. And the students—a shabby, dreary army, shabby in both mind and body. It wasn't thought and culture that characterized the reading room, but cramming, cramming, cramming! You memorized Rohl's history of German literature and set aside books that had over a certain number of pages. Intellectual conversation I heard little of. When the girls weren't discussing the required reading list they were discussing boys and clothes, exactly like at my girls' school, the difference being that here the reading list came first. The reading list and exams. You do pick up a few things when you have people around you the whole day, but I never heard anything interesting. Yet all the same I longed, often, to get closer to them; I went lurking around on the fringes of their obviously confident community.

In high school I'd had a certain position—uncomfortably exposed—so in regards to that it was a relief to disappear into the crowd. But towards the end of high school I'd found a couple of friends—Bente was one. At the University no one sought my company. I was too helpless and shy to take the initiative myself, so I'd been going around alone.

But now that I had Bente, everything was different. It gave me security and self-respect. Even about such a small thing as the daily lunch break in the students' cellar restaurant. Before, I'd sidled in awkwardly, ducking my head, stiff with shyness, hardly daring to glance around. I got into line and didn't look up until I reached the counter. When I'd gotten my hot cocoa I used to sit down anywhere, at the edge of the first table I saw. I always had a book with me and sat and read assiduously while I ate, so that nobody would think I was after their company. I *had* gotten to know some of the Humanities students during the time I'd been there, in the reading room and at lectures. Many of them nodded to me and I nodded back. But I never greeted them first. On the contrary, I always pretended to be very surprised, as if I had just noticed their presence. I was always hurrying, tossing down my food, gulping my hot cocoa, rushing to and from the lecture halls and reading room as if I were incredibly busy and didn't have a second to spare.

But things had changed, now that Bente was around. In the

first place I could be sure there was nothing wrong with me. If I'd had a gaping hole in my stocking heel or a mysterious spot on the back of my dress, she would have seen it and told me. Bente wasn't shy; she didn't mind speaking out. So it couldn't be me the medical students were guffawing at, not me the girls were whispering about. Just appearing in Bente's company gave me new self-confidence. She was so assured and daring, stood out in such a superior way with her dark hair and her beautifully chiseled features. A bit of it rubbed off on me and my drabness too. I no longer hesitated to nod confidently to those I knew, no longer waited for them to recognize me, and even smiled. They could see I wasn't alone, so there couldn't be any misunderstanding. Even so, there were often times when someone sat down at our table and began to talk. Clearly, Bente attracted them. It was pleasant to sit together like that, trading opinions about the reading list and our professors, in that overcrowded, smoke-filled room.

The lunch break, which had been a necessary evil, something to be gotten through, became a high point, a time when I was stimulated, quickened. Sitting in the reading room I could glance at my watch and look forward to lunch. It was the same with the student societies. I'd never set foot into any of them, not even the Humanities Society. Now we went together, Bente and I. I even think that I was the one who suggested we go. It made a pleasant change in the evening. There were lectures and, even if the discussions were often tame and rambling, at least you were part of the group. Not that I took part in any debates—the thought of standing up in the audience and going to the podium alarmed me too much—but I sat together with the other students and it was *our* society. Bente never bothered to stay for the dance. She wanted to go home to bed. And that was a relief. I dreaded sitting alone in a chair while Bente danced. But I was spared that.

There were many recognizable faces from the reading room and lecture halls at these society meetings. We gradually got to know a number of nice people. And it was at lunch in the student cellar that we met Gro for the first time.

I remember it as if it were yesterday. We were there early,

before the worst crush, and found places at a table in the corner nearest the window. We sat eating in peace and quiet, while the cellar resounded with talk and laughter. The cups rattled, the chair legs scraped against the floor, people elbowed and pushed their way forward, and the line stretched away from the counter all the way out the open door.

I remember how good it was to sit so relaxed and to look at the bustle everywhere while I held the thick white cup in both hands, warmed. The ladies behind the counter worked ceaselessly, with swift, busy hands, ladling hot cocoa, pouring coffee and tea, serving Danish pastry, cashiering. More and more people kept coming through the line. A tall young woman left the counter, cup in hand, and wended her way right over to our corner. I'd seen her often, large and radiant, always together with cheerful, boisterous students, usually boys. You couldn't help noticing her. There was something about that big, warm figure that made you want to reach out to her, the way you can't help putting out your hands to a fire. I don't know how it happened, but suddenly I had smiled, even though I didn't know her. And she smiled back, nodded and smiled, taking it as a clear invitation to sit down.

"So nice to find an empty chair. I forgot to take a seat when I got here and then I didn't want to lose my place in line." The words leapt out, eager, breathless, like a brook in spring that can't get to where it's going fast enough. "Lovely to sit down, isn't it?"

It *was* lovely to sit here. I felt my sense of well-being grow more intense, as if it were a spark she'd blown on and gotten to flare up.

"Tell me, haven't we met before?" She leaned towards me with her cup in her hand. "We've noticed each other anyway, haven't we? I'm Gro Holme and I *know* you're Edle Henriksen."

When I think about it now, it seems quite odd—astonishing, to say the least—that she should recognize me. But it didn't seem so at the time. Just natural and warming like everything about Gro.

I can see it in front of me—the dim corner where we sat and, through the fog of smoke, her face shining pale and strangely detached, like a Munch portrait against a background of bluish clouds.

I felt so secure and happy; I could answer her without blushing or stammering. Then I introduced Bente. We talked about the introductory exams Bente was going to take, and Gro told us she was studying minerology and that she was usually up at the Blindern campus, but attended lectures in the city a couple of times a week.

"And you're in Humanities, aren't you?" said Gro to me. "Majoring in history? I've heard you're supposed to be incredibly smart."

Naturally I blushed, twisting in embarrassment and mumbling something about exaggeration and so on. But it seemed different than usual. When other people said things like that I always *felt* my pimples and my whole unfortunate appearance. Being so smart was a wretched mockery. It sounds ridiculous, but that's how it was.

But when Gro said it, it sounded completely different. There was never anything ambiguous about her compliments. I didn't grow embarrassed and ashamed; instead I became wonderfully warm inside. When I close my eyes I can feel it again. There are so few times I've felt happy, truly happy. But at that moment I was . . . I felt so cozy, so relaxed—I didn't want anything beyond that moment. It wasn't torn away from me either, leaving an open wound; it let go gently, sailing away at last like a large shimmering soap bubble.

"I've got to go now," said Gro. "I enjoyed meeting you two. I hope we'll see each other again soon."

We rose too and pushed our way out between the tables. The sky was gray and overcast, but snow was coming and the air was crisp in my lungs.

"Really nice girl," said Bente, looking after Gro. "Seems so open and natural somehow."

That same afternoon we were to meet back at my studio for coffee. Bente came in, thrusting a book parcel at me. "I found a collection of essays by that Mr. Huxley you're so crazy about when I was out buying books. Here you go."

I turned bright red, I think I almost had tears in my eyes—it was like that time she gave me an enamel-four-leaf clover, because I'd helped her study for the final exam.

"Oh, it's nothing, really," Bente said, embarrassed. "You've been a regular pal to me. Letting me live here and everything."

The next time we met at lunch it was Bente who waved Gro over. I would never have dared. She must have so many others whom she knew better and whom she'd rather be together with. But she came right away, smiling as if to old friends. It seemed she was as interested in me as she was in Bente. At least she didn't act any differently. And then I became the one who ended up seeing her most often. It grew into something special. Or maybe it was just me who felt that way, because she came to mean so inordinately much to me. Perhaps she was that way with everyone: familiar, warm-hearted, open. It was part of her personality; she had to be that way.

I would so much like to collect what I know about Gro into a picture. But it's too late. I should have done it before. I no longer remember so clearly. Conversations and moods all flow together. I no longer remember what she told me and what I'm only assuming and concluding through guesses.

I don't remember when it was that she told me about her family. I actually think she didn't say much about them. She'd come from a small coastal town. Both her parents were alive and Gro was the eldest of five children. I remember it struck me as remarkable that Gro had brothers and sisters. She who was so special. But in spite of her warm familiarity there was something solitary about her. I couldn't imagine Gro as a member of a large family, under her parents' authority, fighting with her younger siblings. Money had been tight at home. Her father was a doctor, but he didn't have a large practice. I imagine that he was something of a loafer, but where I get that from, I don't know. Gro never talked disparagingly of her family, and I had the impression that her relationship to them was good one.

38

No, I don't remember clearly enough when she told me *this* and when she said *that*. I mix it up and become completely confused. We sat and talked so many times. But Gro permeates the whole spring—*"wie Wein ausgegossen"* as Rilke says in the *Book of Hours*.

I'll try to describe all of it, bit by bit, and perhaps there'll be a picture at the end. . . .

I can hear that rippling voice: "To be alone is best of all. Can you imagine anything more glorious than to walk in the mountains, completely alone!"

"What do you think about when you're walking up there?" I asked her once, after we'd gotten to know each other better.

I remember her apologetic smile as she answered, "Nothing special. I just walk, just amble along, and feel that everything is just right. And then I look at stones and see if I can find anything interesting. There are so many strange kinds of rock you can happen upon when you're out like that walking. No, when it comes down to it, I never think about anything special then. You know I'm a pragmatist," she said, with a flash of her wide smile. "I'm not as fanciful as you Humanities students, who live in the world of literature."

It wasn't meant as criticism. She was just declaring, That's how you are, this is how I am.

All the same, it hurt. It always hurt when Gro pulled back into herself, where I couldn't follow her. No one knew better than I how immensely far we were from each other, how great the differences. She didn't need to emphasize them.

That's what I said to her once. We were sitting alone in Gro's room and suddenly it slipped out. "Oh Gro, I feel so— inadequate —when you draw back into yourself and shut me out."

"Do I do that?" was all she said. "I don't mean to."

There was a complete silence between us, and the silence grew in me. Now I'd said the one irrevocable thing that would alienate her forever. Now I'd shown my true colors. I was a beggar leeching off other people, displaying my rags. Clothe me! Keep me warm! Demanding and clinging. Bente would have curled her lip in disgust, would have packed her suitcase and left the same day.

"But you have your own world you can close yourself up in," said Gro. "Don't you? You have literature and language, things I don't understand in the least, and your childhood and everything that's happened to you, and the little kernel deep inside that's you alone. Don't you?" she asked again and cocked her head, almost pleadingly.

I wet my lips, but couldn't manage to answer her. Felt how empty and dry I was. I had nothing. . . .

"It's sad you don't have brothers and sisters," she said another time. "They're such good company. Healthy too. You bring each other up."

"Do you think I need bringing up?" I asked drily.

"That's not how I meant it," said Gro, and her voice soothed me, tenderly and a little teasingly. "But it makes you tougher and thicker-skinned."

"Are you so thick-skinned then?"

"Oh, immensely," she answered. "What other people say and do completely rolls off me. I simply couldn't care less."

"That's how Bente is too," I said. "Even though she's an only child with almost no famiy and is rather anti-social at heart. She doesn't give a damn for anything or anybody."

"Really?" said Gro.

There flashed before me Bente's disappointed back. I heard her flat voice, "Have you noticed it's snowing?"

"I'm very interested in people," said Gro. "What they think and believe. About things in general. But not what they think about me."

IV

IT WAS LIKE A SUDDEN, unexpected gift when Gro asked us to her place the first time, rather like when Bente came home with the Huxley book. I was overwhelmed, delighted—and simultaneously plagued by mistrust: Why is she doing this? Is it possible she doen't really have so many others in her life? Maybe she's not what I imagine at all, since she seems content with me . . . But that was just for a moment.

Oh yes, that day: dark and gloomy with yellowish gray fog downtown and the streets brown with slush. It must have been one of those dim raw days at the end of January that reek of the flu. I had a cold at any rate, a stuffed-up head and a sore, red, running nose. I froze in the reading room, couldn't get warm, even though I sat with my ulster around my shoulders and wore thick socks. I probably looked a scarecrow, a vulture, or some kind of large bedraggled bird. It tortured me more than usual, because I couldn't help seeing myself through Bente's eyes. I knew that she loathed people with colds, people with cold sores, who snuffled and blew their noses. I knew that it must be a trial for her—even if she didn't say anything—to sleep in the same room with someone coughing and sneezing the whole night.

I still remember how I lay holding back my cough, *trying* not to cough, but it kept bursting out. I bored my face down into the pillow, lay shaking with soundless explosions, my quilt over my head, stifling and sweating, feeling Bente's irritation almost palpably, just over my head. In a moment the ax

41

would fall— "Edle, *can't* you stop that coughing! You're driving me crazy!" Even though Bente never used to talk to me like that and slept like a log every single night. It was just me who lay there torturing myself for no reason.

"Are you really going out in this disgusting weather, with such a bad cold?" she asked the next morning. She meant it to be thoughtful, but to me it felt like a complaint. "When you're so sick and miserable!"

I had pressed the soaking wet handkerchief to my nose, didn't want her to hear me blow my nose too often.

"As long as I don't give it to you too," I said meekly.

"Oh, I never get colds," said Bente, more than confident.

During the morning I began to revive and by the time Gro came over at lunch, I was feeling much better. She had a cold too; her nose was shiny and red, her voice hoarse, and she wore a thick brown wool scarf around her neck. Her cold had settled in her throat.

Wearing a brown sweater, thin where her elbows rested on the table, Gro put her chin in her hands. "I should go right home and lie down," she said. She just wanted to know if we could come over to her place some evening. "So we could sit around and talk. There's never enough time during these short little lunch breaks. The day after tomorrow maybe? If you two don't have anything else going on." She tilted her head and smiled at me.

I can't explain what swept over me, strong and hot, like nothing I'd ever felt—yes, it was passion. I loved her. All of her. The brown-gold tousled mop of hair, the eyes with dancing flecks of light, the smile, the mouth . . . the brown, threadbare elbows of her sweater. And it rips through me, how she's no longer alive. How she's dead and gone.

But you can't say it aloud. Passion. Because then people immediately suspect something repulsive, sick, perverse. Maybe it is. Maybe I am. Maybe that's what's wrong with me. *Kit* hinted I was. Oh God, how I flinched that time; I felt everything had become sullied, ugly. But even if she were right, so what? Yes, so what!

The one thing I'm sure of is that I've never loved anyone like

I did Gro. If the sexual urge is one of the basic motivations of humanity, then maybe it's gotten warped in me because it never was allowed a natural outlet. There was that pitiful episode with Hans Jørgen, the episode that ended so shamefully. Could it have become something real and true? Impossible to say now. I'm not capable of remembering anything but the shame and humiliation. That's what I have to go through again, in order to be finished with it once and for all.

But that there was anything warped or unhealthy about my love for Gro—yes, I believed it myself by the end; it tortured me like so many other things. Now I see it all differently. I can't believe it was wrong—the strongest, most complete feeling I've ever known. My only love. I wonder how many women feel like that, while hiding or disguising it? For aren't these just the feelings that breathe from Sappho's poems, and aren't her songs counted among the most beautiful and noble in the literature of the world?

I must have felt that day that I loved her. That foul gray day shone, because she sat there smiling at me.

I've told myself that Gro symbolized life to me, that she was the single truly harmonious person I've ever known, so completely in accord with life itself—that that was what attracted me. Perhaps I was fooling myself. Perhaps the whole thing was bound up with a perverse sexual urge. But is it right to complain of something growing warped, to be ashamed of it in silent humiliation, to brood over it for eight years, without asking why? If I knew why, perhaps it wouldn't seem so warped. One way or another you have to grow.

Gro was renting a room at the top of an old, decrepit brick apartment building up by Majorstua. It was a corner building, with towers and cornices and mock ornamentation, the kind of thing this city is crawling with, a discouraging reminder of dark green plush and the naturalism of the 1880s: Albertine, the poor prostitute, the seamstresses in the novels of Jonas Lie.

We climbed up worn, brown stairs, where it smelled of cabbage and fat frying; we read the faint brass plates and soiled name cards. There seemed to be tenants on every floor. At the top we found the narrow white card that said, "Gro Holme,

43

student." I remember how my heart sank: Gro living here! I had the bourgeois itch to organize, to catalogue. Probably still do. And when reality doesn't jibe with my card file, I get confused and feel duped. Perhaps it's normal to react like that. What do I know? I know so little about people. I can imagine Kit is like that, wanting everything—people, events—just her way. But she also has the gift of seeing things exactly as she wants them to be, and is therefore never disappointed.

I had imagined Gro's surroundings so differently. Light, beautiful—an old-fashioned white wooden house with a garden and spacious, sunny rooms—the way I still think of her home in the small town where she grew up. But it shouldn't have surprised me to find it was dark and over-furnished. Things have a tendency to be like that—incongruous—to bristle and bulge when you try to press them into contrived stereotypes.

The grimy, dim entrance felt oppressive. We'd come from the quiet and purity of a snowy evening into this atmosphere reeking of cabbage. That's *not* how it should have been.

Bente rang the bell and Gro came to open the door—still wearing a wool scarf around her neck. I'd changed earlier, had put on a dark blue, long-sleeved silk dress. I grew painfully embarrassed when I saw her standing there in her usual checked skirt and threadbare brown sweater. Bente had changed because I had; she'd put on a bright red silk blouse instead of the red sweater she wore every day. Here we were, all decked out and full of expectation, like two country cousins. And there was nothing. It had all been imaginary. She'd flung out a casual, "Come on over," and right away I'd jumped at it, because I was stupid and boring and unaccustomed to going anywhere. And I'd included Bente in my foolishness. How angry she'd be! It was fairly obvious that Gro had forgotten she'd invited us. That's what I thought. But all that hurt suspiciousness vanished in an instant.

"So *nice* of you to come," said Gro, and it sounded as if she were happy about it. She brushed the dry snow off our ulsters. "Look at your stars!" And there really were little stars—light as down, shimmering—melting on our collars and sleeves.

44

We followed her through a narrow dark entryway that smelled of wet wool and into a brightly lit room.

"Please come in," said Gro.

It was a small square room under a mansard roof, with a high, narrow window facing the street. Looking back now, there's a warm, festive sheen over the little room—like a room in a dream, golden and permeated with warmth and Gro's smile.

But that first time I was disappointed, I remember. Naturally I was spoiled, being used to Alfred Bugge's carpets and Gobelin tapestries. My own little studio apartment, which I thought so spartan, was luxurious compared to Gro's room. It wasn't just simple, it was naked and ugly. The white globe lamp in the ceiling shone as garishly as the light in a waiting room, over bare yellow walls, on to an iron bed with brass knobs, an iron heating stove, a folding screen and a washstand. The window gaped, a black rectangle in the wall. In front of it stood a table and three chairs. Over the bed, bookshelves of bleached pine had been put up. Mainly books on minerology—I found that out later. Gro never read anything else. On the bed lay a patchwork quilt and a couple of colorful pillows. The quilt and the pillows and books were the only personal belongings there. It could just as well have been a room in a cheap little hotel.

But the table was set. Set with three red-checked placemats and a large, round ceramic bowl full of buns. And it smelled delightfully of coffee.

"You look so nice," said Gro, laying my ulster on the bed. "I really thought of changing, but I got home so late. I barely managed to get the coffee ready. And then there's this miserable cold that doesn't want to give up. You're almost better off in your regular old clothes when you feel so chilly and shivery."

She seated us on either side of her and lit the red candles in the wrought-iron candlesticks on the table.

"Now I'll turn off the light in the ceiling—it'll be much cozier."

And it actually became quite cozy. The yellow walls, fold-

45

ing screen, stove—all those ugly, bare things—faded away in a soft, dusky darkness. It was just the three of us in a world closed and snug. I can see it before me—the candlelight falling softly over the red-checked mats, the yellow butter on the buns. Tiny fires flickered in the uncurtained black window.

"Isn't it pretty with the snow?" asked Gro.

I pressed my forehead against the cold moist glass, looked out over the rooftops where the snow whirled white under the dark, starry sky. On the windowsill was a white hyacinth that gave off a quiet fragrance.

Gro poured coffee into our cups and a thick brown liqueur from a stoneware jug into small, colored glasses.

"Let's start with liqueur, shall we? It's strong and good, if I do say so myself. I got it from a friend. He makes it himself."

The words grated. I was suddenly back in high school, hearing the lazy voice of Tove, the frivolous class beauty. She sat on a desk, swinging her legs, and extended a languid hand with a wide, gold-colored bracelet. "Isn't this divine? A friend gave it to me." While I stood there, thin and ungainly with a frozen smile—like an old maid at a ball.

Obviously Gro had male friends—many of them. And why shouldn't she prefer one in particular? Be in love, just like other people, think of getting engaged! What was more natural? But the thought was still offensive. Gro in love—with stupid, mooning eyes—eagerly aflutter to please a man. Male friends, well certainly . . . But that she should have a crush on one of them, let him kiss her, maybe be rejected, walked all over, that she should cry into her pillow . . . Gro who was so free!

Then Bente asked, straight out, "Are you engaged, Gro?"

I winced over her asking that way and couldn't help leaning closer to catch the answer—as if I were afraid Gro was going to whisper it to Bente and I wouldn't hear.

"No . . ." said Gro slowly. "No, not really." She smiled in her quick, droll way. "I have a friend at home. He's a dentist. We've been together since our school days. He's two years older than me. Now he's started a practice at home. But he doesn't like me studying. He's a little old-fashioned that way, and that's really too bad, because I can't imagine quitting."

Well, well, I thought maliciously. He wants to, but she doesn't. That's how it should be. She was putting her studies first, not flinging everything aside; she didn't come running whenever he called. In my heart I gloated over the dentist. Saw him humbled, begging and beseeching. And Gro with her little half-smile, "No, I'm so sorry . . ."

"You shouldn't get married," said Bente gloomily. "You'll just be suffocated."

Gro put her cup down and looked at Bente in smiling surprise. I see her—as clearly as I did then. Yes, now I really see her . . . the curly brown-gold mop of hair, the slightly tilted happy eyes. She had a cleft in her chin—I'd forgotten that—and a dimple in one cheek. Her chin is small and round with the hint of a double chin. Strange how alive she is for me at this moment—so alive it aches. It's the smile that does it, that astonishing smile, that *was* Gro. It appears before me, exactly like . . . what does it remind me of? Something I've seen, read . . . A picture . . .

The Cheshire Cat! All of a sudden I have it. The cat in *Alice in Wonderland*! How tasteless. But Gro really does remind me of the big plush cat.

And by the end only the smile was left. The cat had disappeared, but Alice saw the smile plainly against the sky.

It's been many years since I read that storybook. I can't say it made any great impression on me. It was just nonsense, as far as I recall. But this grotesque image—the Cheshire Cat who smiled from ear to ear—has still been in my unconscious all these years, and now it helps me to remember Gro.

That shocks me. It's grotesque, unseemly. You shouldn't remember a dead friend like that. I should have something else with which to hold her fast, a beautiful portrait, something noble and grandiose. But the Cheshire Cat and its endlessly gleaming smile won't leave me. Gro's smile—that wide luminous smile. How alive it makes her seem suddenly. How near.

She put her cup down and looked at Bente. "Are you speaking from experience?"

"Yes, I am," Bente said drily.

And I thought, Here we go—now we're going to get Bente's whole story. I remembered that first evening, when she sat telling it to me until far into the night. I didn't want to hear it again. It didn't concern me any longer. She took it from me and gave it to Gro.

But as it happened I did Bente an injustice—strange how often I've done that. She seemed to be tired of her own story, and gave only a brief version of her marriage and life in Lillevik.

"Good heavens, I didn't imagine you were married," interrupted Gro. She sat with her chin in her hands and looked at Bente with sparkling eyes.

After a moment she said, "You don't mean to tell me you have a *child*! A child you carried and brought into the world!"

But Bente just looked down at her brown, boyish fists and kept talking, flatly and monotonously.

"Oh, Bente, how *could* you leave him!" wailed Gro. "Your own little boy. Of course he *needs* you!"

All of a sudden it struck me that what Bente had done was terrible. And I had encouraged her. What must Gro think of me! In a minute she'd turn those flashing eyes on me—You mean little egotist! Taking a little child from his own mother! How *could* you?

But Bente looked steadily at her hands and mumbled, "He's not mine. He belongs to the Arnesen family. They've annexed him, every little bit."

"Oh Bente," said Gro, half-groaning, half-laughing. "You're just like one of those little birds that won't go back to sitting on her eggs because someone has touched them."

Bente looked up with flaming cheeks.

"Have you really decided to abandon the battlefield just like that, Bente? If you have something against your in-laws you definitely shouldn't let them have him."

"That's not what I've decided," said Bente irascibly. "I'll go back and get him when I've made something of myself and can be something to him. Now I'm just jelly," she snapped.

"This is almost like Nora in the *Doll's House*," smiled Gro. "But I've never thought of you as a 'lark.'"

"Yes, Nora left three kids and she still gets all the applause," said Bente bitterly. "On stage you have permission to be true to yourself. But god help the person who tries it in real life."

Gro sighed and smiled. She opened her mouth as if to say something but closed it again and shook her head.

"I think I'd be crazy about a child if I had one," she said finally. "I'd start pampering it something awful. Have it on my lap the whole day, against all good child-rearing advice."

She shook her head and smiled to herself.

"And your studies?" Bente asked scornfully.

"Yes . . . my studies, you're right. Of course you'd have to be finished with them." She mused over this with her chin propped up on her hands. "First you'd have to have every-thing ready, and have made a warm, feathered nest. And then nine months to prepare yourself—slowly, solemnly." She broke off with her droll smile. "How amazing to feel it grow-ing inside."

"The first three months all I did was throw up," said Bente. "And then I blew up like a balloon. I waddled around. Almost couldn't tie my shoelaces. And everyone was so considerate!" She made a face.

We sat awhile without saying anything. At last Gro gath-ered her thoughts again and smiled at me. "What about you, Edle? Wouldn't you like to have children?"

"And with whom am I supposed to have children?"

Those words coursed through me like a snake's poisonous venom in my blood. But I didn't say them aloud. Not then. I turned bright red, sat there like a statue and pressed my lips together. I hadn't learned yet to close up, quick as a flash, behind a smooth exterior. I was still torn between two impos-sibilities: I couldn't hide what I felt and lacked the courage to say it.

But I remember another, later time. It was also at Gro's place, but we were alone. And Gro asked, just like the first time, "Edle, you'd like to have children too, wouldn't you?"

Then I barked it out. "And with whom am I supposed to have children?" And got angry at myself, because there were tears in my eyes. It was shameful. And at the same time it was a

49

relief to set it down in front of Gro, like a dog setting down a stick at the foot of its master.

"Of course you can have children," said Gro. "If you just want to yourself. If you just want it badly enough. But you have to want it, want it with your whole heart. Let yourself blossom."

I stiffened. Laughter would come now, a raw roar of laughter that would knock everything down. Blossom!

But Gro's face shone in the twilight. She stood staring out the window, over the black rooftops, to where the sunset smouldered. And her face glowed radiantly.

It wasn't me she was thinking about. She was far away—in the midst of the sunset's red yearning, deep in the warm darkness of her own being.

I felt a sudden evil desire to rip the smile from that radiant face, to extinguish the glow.

"Blossom? What do you think I am, a flower?" I asked coldly, and stared at her as if I'd just operated and cut straight down to the bone. Her smile died, abruptly extinguished. That's exactly what I wanted—only the knife lodged in my own flesh.

I remember one time as a child. I was quite young, sitting with pencil and paper—I wanted to draw a horse and couldn't get it right. I struggled and kept drawing new figures—but none of them looked like horses. And than I looked up at Grandma. She was nearby, smiling kindly. Perhaps I asked her to help me. At any rate she took the pencil, made some strokes, stopped, drew again, and there was a horse, clearly a horse, with head, mane, hooves, and a long, shaggy tail. "Here you are, dear, here's your horse!" And she handed me the drawing. I can't explain it, but suddenly I took the pencil and began to scribble all over the horse, that fine horse, with hard, unsteady strokes, harder and harder, while my tears dripped on the paper. "That's not the way it was supposed to be," I kept mumbling, even though it was finer than I'd dreamed of, finer than I could ever manage to draw it. Harder and harder I scribbled, until the pencil snapped. And it hurt me, hurt me so much that Grandma only smiled.

But Gro didn't smile.

"I don't think you care about children, Edle," she said mildly. "You only want to be like other people."

She continued to look out the window and again she was far away.

But that was later, many weeks later. It must have been in February sometime, because it was before I met Hans Jørgen. That first evening at Gro's was more peaceful. And Gro hadn't gotten so close to me that I would dream of hurting her. Apart from that one painful moment when I stiffened with shame, everything was harmonious. The sudden question hadn't been meant unkindly, I saw that. Gro wouldn't say anything wounding.

That first evening—how good I felt. The snow sparkled so quietly, the red candles burned, and Gro's smile shone towards me. I thought, if I could have Gro as a friend, a real, true friend, that would be enough. I wouldn't ask for more.

But afterwards . . . that wasn't enough. I can't remember being truly satisfied afterwards. I was always on my toes after something more.

Is it always that way? With everyone? I wish I knew more about people, besides the trivial, superficial things—I wish I knew something essential about each and every person. Perhaps others know it, everyone except me. And what's the essential thing in *me*? Layer after layer of thought and acquired ideas, complexes, memories, inhibitions and, deep inside, a shriveled-up seed that long ago lost its growing power.

"You two must come again," said Gro. "Very soon—won't you?" She stood in the open doorway and waved good-bye to us as we went down the dirty, dim staircase. Her words continued to ring in my ears the whole way home, through the snow-quiet, deserted streets. "So nice to meet people like you—I know so few girls here—there are mostly boys at Blindern—and there's something special about girlfriends. . . ."

Bente didn't speak until we were outside our own door.

"Gro is really an okay person and all that. But she's a little too illogical and inconsistent to be a scientist. One minute lecturing us about kids like they were alpha and omega. And the next second admitting how she herself didn't want to give up her studies."

"She probably meant she wanted to be finished with one before she started on the other," I said shortly. Bente had no right to criticize Gro.

"And put it all away in a drawer when she gets married?" Bente grumbled.

"Gro is marvelous," I said vehemently, and put the key in the lock. Felt how red my cheeks were.

"Yes, that's exactly *why*," Bente said, lamely, and looked at me in wonder.

I hurried to open up, and we didn't say much more. We were tired and went straight to bed.

After that evening things weren't the same with Bente. The change probably started then. Naturally it went in stages— unnoticeable to begin with, but after a few weeks you could plainly feel it. By the time I parted from Bente at Easter break it had become a completely different relationship than during the first agitated month, when I tiptoed around her and didn't dare cough at night.

I continued to like her until the very last day. But I no longer groveled in admiration. On the contrary; I gradually became quite critical and wasn't afraid to show it. When I think back on it, we did have what I'd always dreamed of—a true, frank friendship, with both of us on an equal footing. And I let it go, just like that. What an idiot I was! And now it's too late.

How Bente felt about it is hard to tell. One result of the change between us is that I stopped being so absorbed in her. I no longer watched anxiously for her every little reaction to what I said and did. But I don't think she noticed a change anyway. I remember it stung me a few times that she could be just like before, while I'd become so different. But why should she have noticed anything! She's never been sensitive, has never been used to analyzing feelings either—her own or other peoples'. And from the first moment I'd exerted myself to appear exactly as balanced and level-headed towards her as I later really became.

52

If she felt anything at all, it must have been closer to relief. She abhorred having people cling to her and valued a frank, unsentimental attitude.

What occupied her were simple, concrete questions. Should she go back to Sven, or should she stay in Oslo and get herself an education? What about the boy? What about the family? I could see her grappling daily with these problems, even though she didn't talk about them. She was often preoccupied, sitting with a wrinkled forehead, smoking cigarette after cigarette. She was studying as well—not hectically as in the first weeks, but stubbornly, persistently. She took long ski trips by herself and came home completely worn out, to sink down in a chair with her legs flung out. In such moments she appeared almost content.

Bente wasn't one to arrive at things abstractly. She had to feel a way of life in her body, try first one way, then another, like someone trying on shoes. Walk a few steps, stop, see if they pinched—that was the most important thing—that they didn't pinch. If they did, presto, they were off and another pair on. Maybe they'd fit better.

I felt sorry for Bente. If she'd been a boy the opportunities would have been greater; she could have gone to sea, gotten drunk in foreign ports, fought, roistered, loved. Instead all she had was marriage to try on and then kick off.

But never mind Bente's bad luck then. A year later she had all the opportunities in the world—and she made use of them! The five years of war must have been like one long, thrilling steeplechase—Bente jumping with flying colors, all warm and spent, with red cheeks and eyes shining from speed and excitement . . .

She lives at home in Lillevik now, with Sven and the boy. and everything is just fine, so they say. Bente goes on creating breathing room for herself. No one dares to say "little Bente" anymore. When she says, "lie down," all of them lie down flat together, and the Arnesen family flattest of all, at a respectful distance. For old Arnesen was, well, not exactly a collaborator, but—he waffled a little. And Mrs. Arnesen got hysterical when the Germans came to arrest Bente and denounced her daughter-in-law in indignant, Lillevik-accented German. So now she can never say "*little*" with the same motherly protectiveness. She doesn't dare utter a syllable about the suffering and fear she went through for Bente's sake. For all her sleepless nights and dark hours are worth absolutely nothing in contrast to the glorious contribution Bente made. Sven, who was imprisoned in Grini for two years as a hostage for his wife, has atoned for the rest of his family and can be accepted as a husband. But he doesn't dare fuss over or coddle his "little wife" because that would seem ridiculous.

Mrs. Holt at the school, who is from Lillevik, has told me this. Whether it's really like that, I don't know. It may be completely different. Sven may be the one to break out next time. Or perhaps Bente has been through so much that she's learned to be humble. What do I know?

I haven't seen any of them since that spring eight years ago. All I know is that Bente's name exploded in letters of fire across the land. Naturally she is another person today than the restless young Bente who sat in my room smoking evening after evening while she stockpiled ammunition.

V

FEBRUARY CAME AND WENT like a short golden dream. How gladly I'd exchange my ordinary life for that one month. Not in order to relive any special event. Nothing *happened*. It was all in the atmosphere—a spring-blue, trembling feeling—a glow cast over everyday life.

It feels so far away, that time—my happiest time—like an Atlantis sunk in the sea, hidden in memory. Pictures jump out, clear and sharp, yet, all the same, astonishingly strange. It's like looking at old photographs. You see them and wonder: Is this me? Did I really look like that? Was that the way I was once?

We sit on the steps of Domus Media with our lunch sacks, Bente and I, and turn our faces up to the sun in enjoyment. I can still feel the sun's warmth on my eyelids and the trembling dark red color inside. The feeling follows me into the dim reading room. I feel faint, disoriented, light-headed, as if I'm intoxicated.

Sometimes Gro is with us, sitting right between us, crunching on a raw carrot, stretching her legs in her sturdy boots, throwing bread crumbs to the fat pigeons that strut over the square. It's dripping and melting around us; law students kick wads of paper around; the little park behind us smells spring-like, of sun and newly thawed earth.

Or perhaps we stroll across the square arm in arm, letting the sun bake our backs. Cold gusts of wind blow from the shadows but we keep away from them and walk in the sun. We talk about feminism and Madame Curie and the Greek comedy and the myth of the logos and what fun it would be to know Greek. Something thaws in me. Everything read and studied, that I otherwise keep locked in my brain, deep frozen for use in some future exam, melts and streams forth. Like ice breaking up. I talk myself into a white heat, about the polis and the bureaucracy of the Roman empire, and what was frozen glows and comes alive in the warm, spring sun.

"It's so much fun to listen to you, Edle," said Gro. "You know, novels and poetry aren't my cup of tea. I don't understand much about them. But history—I'm with you there! When you become a professor, I'll go to all your lectures and sit in the first row and take notes. What fun it will be, when we 'go hear Edle Henriksen.'"

And Bente sighed, envying us who had come so far.

"It's too damn disgusting that anybody has to struggle with this introductory shit. By the time I've managed to claw my way up to the junior class, Edle will probably be in full swing with her doctorate."

We often joked about my doctorate. At the time it seemed so obvious that we would continue at the University, keep on studying, pursuing knowledge. Teaching in high school was never mentioned at all—perhaps was a possibility for Bente—but absolutely not for Gro and me.

And now I've ended up as a teacher in a girls' school! It was the war that did it. I'm no educator, I should never have become a teacher. But the University was closed after I'd gotten my degree. I'd completely lost any pleasure in my studies anyway and was growing tired. The main thing was to be finished and independent.

But now . . . Perhaps I could begin again, take up where I left off. I'm only thirty, after all. If I could only recapture the pure, sparkling joy of work, the joy of mastering a subject, of researching, pushing my way into a new and unknown land!

To a certain extent that was probably what illuminated that long ago happy time, the fresh happiness of studying—of using your powers, extending yourself, feeling that you were growing.

I'm giving a talk—on Bjørnson and Czechoslovakia. I, who hate to be in the limelight, have voluntarily taken the task on. I am so horribly nervous; my voice trembles and stutters; the auditorium swims before my eyes. It's packed full; it's always full for these practice lectures. But the talk is good. I know it's good. I've collected material for several weeks and prepared extra hard.

And when it's all over, the professor comes over and thanks me and compliments me for the quite excellent talk. Several students ask if they can borrow the manuscript. And Gro is enthusiastic. Both she and Bente attended. Gro talks heatedly about the partition of Czechoslovakia and how outrageous it is. I don't understand anything about it. Current politics is something I don't pay much attention to. But of course it's a pity about the Czechs.

How far away that feels and yet, all the same, how much alive. Gro sticks her arm under mine and talks eagerly; the warm, happy face is close to mine, the slightly tilted eyes beam. And out of the window of the auditorium Bente hangs, a dark head, a dashing red sweater; she waves and calls to us, "coming right away." The military band marches down the street on its way to the castle. The brass sparkles, booming and tinkling, rhythmic, festive. Sunshine, springtime.

I remember an early February evening with inflamed red clouds in the sky and a bloody reflection in the streets. Bente sat at the desk and crammed Latin, crushing her head between her hands as if threatening it to hold on to each new word. It was almost dark in the room. The study lamp shone, yellow and rational, on the littered desk, over the dictionary and gloss book and the thin little blue notebook that was the heart of it all—the Latin text. Bente quoted grandiloquently, letting the words roll off her tongue, enjoying herself. And then with an arrogant toss of the head, "They hang high, said the fox . . . . Can't you see old Cicero sitting there and drooling impotently over the *voluptatem* while mumbling so sanctimoniously about the *senecute!*" She made a face. "The joys of old age. Pah!"

I had to smile. That was the amusing thing about Bente. She totally lacked the prevailing cynical attitude about cramming for the preparatory exam. What she read always came alive for her. And Cicero's purported hypocrisy infuriated her more than the convoluted syntax. I took it upon myself to defend him. How tragic—a great man and then to be broken on the wheel and patted on the shoulder throughout history, compassionately seen through by narrow-minded students who only had their callow youth to weigh against his knowledge, his political and cultural position—and that callow youth had all the advantage! Something pained me suddenly, while outside the sunset flamed. The window was like an illuminated red rectangle, an irrational stain, that defied reason's yellow light.

I was restless and couldn't concentrate. I had to go out. Patches of ice scrunched under my feet. I walked on, with my hands balled up in my ulster pockets, with my heart banging so strangely, heavy and painful.

There was a light in Gro's window. She was home then. I trudged up the worn stairs with expectation hammering in my blood. It gnawed like hunger.

The stranger who opened the door was a new Gro, one I'd never seen before. She wore a long-sleeved, floor-length black velvet dress that clung tightly to her breasts and thighs and then fell in heavy folds. My expectation froze momentarily. Inopportune, obtrusive . . . I shouldn't have come.

There was a fine blush on her pale cheeks and her generous mouth shone boldly red. In the square-cut décolleté her skin gleamed matte and white, strangely naked against the black velvet. She looked like a lady of the manor from the Middle Ages, high-bosomed, delicate-skinned, chaste and sinful at the same time. And I thought suddenly, This is how men see her. Perhaps this is how she *is*. But no, no, the true Gro is the one who studies minerology, who tramps around in a skirt and sweater and big boots and likes best of all to be alone. All the same I heard her, with painful clarity, "I think I'd be crazy about a child if I had one." And, "Let yourself blossom, Edle! Blossom!"

I mumbled an apology, wanting to turn and leave immediately, but Gro extended both hands and pulled me inside.

"Oh, Edle, won't you come in? I don't have to go quite yet, so we can sit and chat a minute . . . how nice!"

Crumbs, poor crumbs. She must have felt how disappointed I was, for she turned quite solicitous, pulled me down on the bed and sat next to me with her hand resting on mine, talking in a rippling voice that caressed and smoothed over everything rough and prickly, while managing in a strange way to stay her usual Gro self, in spite of the velvet and the make-up.

"How annoying that I have to go out tonight. There's a party at Blindern, you see. Nothing so terribly exciting, but it's always enjoyable to see the other students. Probably a couple of professors will come too." Her voice rippled on.

I was strangely struck. Gro was so open, as open as Bente; she never made a secret of anything, never acted mysterious; she was full of ordinarly common sense, candor itself. Yet all the same I knew so little about her; I stood outside and stared blindly at a closed, locked door.

We're so isolated! Poets and lovers have complained for centuries about the absolute loneliness of the soul. All the same, we never learn; we struggle and strain to climb out of the depths of our egos and stare hungrily at other people's lives— the way I did with Gro that spring. I stretched out my frozen hands to the warmth of the bonfire, knowing that in a few moments it would be over, that I would be alone again.

"I'm going to Svalbard* this summer," said Gro. "You want to come? No, you'd rather go to Rome or Greece."

"I would, if you'd come," I answered and thawed a little.

Oh yes, that's something Gro would enjoy, getting out and taking a look around. So much to see and learn. The mere thought drove her wild. Her eyes shone. And I was ashamed of my foreign sojourns—how little I'd seen of people and daily life. I'd sat in my room and read, had gone to museums.

"Germany is where I'd really like to go," Gro said seriously.

---

*A group of Norwegian islands in the Arctic Ocean, of which the largest is Spitsbergen.

"It would be interesting to see what's actually going on there. It sounds so awful. No, I wouldn't mind a trip to Germany."

They are words that sink down and then bob up again with a new and horrible meaning. They came back to me during the war when the convoy ships blasted their horns out in the harbor, when I heard, purely by accident on the street one day, that Gro had just been sent away. "Germany is where I'd really like to go."

I'd spent half a year in Munich. I remember how interested she was. How many questions she asked. But I'd seen nothing more than order and clean streets—and the museums, of course.

"I have to go now," apologized Gro. "I'm meeting him under the clock at seven thirty."

Which him? She would certainly have told me if I'd asked. But I didn't ask. Didn't want to know. Didn't care to hear about the boys at Blindern and the part of her life that didn't include me. I stayed sitting in her room awhile, glanced into a newspaper that lay on the table. Then I turned off the lights and went quickly down the stairs, hoping against hope to find her outside, a solitary figure in floor-length black, hoping that something had happened and that the party had been called off. But the street was deserted and empty. All I could do was return home.

I found Bente on fire with enthusiasm for Nietzsche. She'd given up on Cicero and lay on her stomach on the bed in her red bathrobe, with *The History of Philosophy* open on her pillow. As soon as she saw me she cried out.

"'All due respect to governesses, but isn't it time that Philosophy gave up its faith in governesses?' Isn't that great!"

Why hadn't I told her about Nietzsche? Was it maybe because some hypocritical killjoys had gotten together to suppress him?

I answered that she couldn't have gotten that impression from *The History of Philosophy* because he took up as much space there as Father Kant himself.

"But he's not required reading!" said Bente triumphantly. Tomorrow she was going to the university library to get hold of Zarathustra. Bente—with her German!

I reeled off some poisonous sarcasm on the subject of "the blond Beast" and the "crucified Dionysius." Perhaps it came off coarser than I intended, because I remember that Bente stared and said, "Boy, you're mad! What's eating you?"

"I can't stand lunatic ravings," I answered shortly, but at the same time felt I'd gotten it off my chest.

Afterwards we had a good time chatting till late in the evening. Bente brought the teapot out and served hard rolls with butter and brown goat cheese. We sat with our legs curled under us on the sofa, crunching on the rolls and sipping the glowing-hot tea.

"I wonder if there's going to be a war," said Bente. "It's so damned disgusting that he just moves in wherever he feels like it. Now *he's* a real lunatic! But he must have something, the way he can get people to crawl on their bellies when he says Boo."

I remember I maintained that the war *had* to come, but that I didn't actually believe my own words.

"Nah, nothing will come of it," said Bente impatiently. "They yield and yield and at the end what happened to the toad will happen to him. He'll swell up and blow himself to bits."

Her voice rang with bitterness, with the disgust of an active person who lives in a world where nothing happens.

Now I'm recalling another incident, when Gro was at our place. We sat drinking tea, once again, and suddenly Gro asked, "What's your little boy called, Bente?"

"Harald."

"After your father?" I asked, astonished—so astonished that Gro looked at me.

"Is that so strange?" she asked.

With Bente sitting there it wasn't easy to explain—that she and her father—and especially now he was dead. At a loss, I stammered something and was relieved when Bente interrupted.

"Father and I were at loggerheads. It was a real pity, because we should have stuck together. But all I was was a little brat—all the time. Everything I did was wrong. We didn't see much of each other either. Father never had time. He was a doctor who lived for the operating table."

"My father is a doctor too," said Gro with laughing eyes, "but for the most part he plays the violin. Unfortunately I didn't inherit his musical abilities. I can't hold a note."

"He's probably at home a lot then, isn't he? My father never was. And those few times he was, he always thought he should be teaching me manners. Boy, we had some scenes!"

"But now, since he . . ." said Gro carefully. "You'd probably like for the boy to. . . ."

"Well, yes," Bente shrugged. "Oh, about the name, you mean?" She laughed a little. "It was mostly because the whole Arnesen family expected him to be christened Sven. All they were calling him was Little Sven or Sven Junior. Disgusting. I didn't say anything—before the christening itself. Then I calmly christened him Harald. You can imagine what a hullabaloo that caused. The church was chock-full. All of Lillevik was there, and the pastor was a cousin of my mother-in-law. He had the name all ready to spit out. 'What is the child to be called?' he asked. 'Harald,' I answered. I didn't have a godmother for him, I was carrying him myself—I'd gotten my way with *that*. 'Harald,' loud and clear. There wasn't a hope of calling him Sven after that."

I couldn't help laughing. It was just like Bente. Gro sat with her chin resting on her hands and smiled.

"What about Sven?" I asked maliciously.

"Oh, Sven." She made a face. "You know what happened? Nothing at all, my girl. The minute we came home from church I had to go into the kitchen and talk to the cook—god knows why, she always did it her way in the end. The nanny dealt with the baby, gave him his bottle and so forth—I've never had a drop of milk. And when I returned to the guests Sven had gone around and told them that *he* had tried hard to persuade me but I hadn't wanted to. It was only that morning that I'd finally decided to give in and call the boy Harald! What do you think of that! Namely that *he* thought all that business with Little Sven and Sven Junior was silly and *he* admired his father-in-law so much—that's true, actually, he was damned impressed by Father."

"But later . . . when the two of you were alone?"

"Oh, it's no use. Sven is like an eel. Whatever you say and do, it's no use." She shook herself like a wet dog. "Even if you kick up a gigantic fuss, it all settles down again, you can count on it, and is just the same as before: 'Bente, sweet girl. Sven's clever little wife.' Oh, definitely."

I'd forgotten the whole episode, But now I recall it clearly, word for word, as well as Bente's irritated tone. But at the same time there was—this sounds unbelievable—there was actually something admiring in her voice. It struck me as she was talking, just like that time she mentioned Hitler ("He must have something."). It makes me wonder how it is now. Have the shards of the last violent upheaval fallen down to settle into the same old pattern? Is it possible that Sven, once again and in spite of everything, has come out ahead?

"Anyway, the boy's name is Harald," said Bente with a crooked smile.

"And if your father had lived and you'd stayed in Oslo," said Gro, still with her chin in her hands, "the boy probably would have had a third name—one that could have annoyed *him*."

Bente looked a little surprised, then she asked, and it amazed me to hear her sound so meek, "Do you think I'm childish?"

"No, of course not," said Gro, warm and contrite. "I think you're sweet. The way you are, you probably need an outburst now and then."

Once a week I had dinner with Mama and Alfred. I still do, whenever they're at home and I don't have a good excuse. But I remember that spring there was something cozy about those "family dinners." I was no longer the gray mouse who lived at home—a fixture that had to be acknowledged simply because it was there. I came as a guest and was treated with all the goodwill and interest that guests received in Alfred Bugge's house. Of course it wasn't Mama and Alfred who had changed. It was me behaving more freely that affected their attitude, so that they also became more spontaneous with me. I had liberated myself, put them at a distance, and with that the whole relationship shrank to normal proportions: Miss Henriksen visiting Mr. and Mrs. Bugge. Well, maybe it's not so normal for a relationship between a mother and stepfather and their only daughter to be so lukewarm. But in our case it is. Why not take what's offered and make the best of it. Why force the woman up on a pedestal in an artificial position as "Edle's mother" when she is an excellent Mrs. Bugge?

Everything turned out splendidly that spring. I didn't think much about it—my relationship to her had become of secondary importance, but now that I'm back to where I was before, barricaded behind the old hostile criticism, now I wonder . . . and I remember that time with—yes, with a certain nostalgia.

I can't judge Mama with any degree of fairness. I always have the gnawing sensation that she's betrayed me on some central issue. But which one? She made a good home for me, made sure I received the clothes and equipment that were suitable for every occasion. Via Alfred she sent me to a private school, to the University, on expensive stays abroad. It annoyed her, as a matter of fact, that I was so "inexpensive to operate"; she would gladly have showered me with furs and jewelry—as if that could have helped.

She herself believes she is an excellent mother—and perhaps she is. She has *tried* hard to be one at any rate. She's never had to try hard to be a good wife to Alfred. That came naturally to her, from the first minute. It wasn't her fault that I got to be too much for her to handle, that I didn't resemble her one bit, but instead took after my father, the remote, serious associate professor. That I developed into someone unusually ugly and intelligent. *She's* the one with the right to be disappointed over her hideous failure of a daughter, who has been the cause of so many annoyances, and who criticizes her on top of it all. Yet all the same she's tried her best to take it with good humor.

Mosse Bugge is well-meaning and superficial. She likes pretty clothes and good food and society and a little wine and a little innocent flirting. She's never cross and she does wish other people well—as long as she's doing better herself. There's no evil in her. And at least she makes Alfred happy.

From a distance I can see it all, her good sides and her little weaknesses. Why is it then that as soon as I get together with her, there's a short circuit? The intense antipathy flames up, breaking every connection between us. Is it envy? Jealousy? An old Oedipus complex? I can't find any reasonable explanation—perhaps because it goes so far back, is entangled with my childhood memories—it has entered my bloodstream and become a part of me.

As long as I can remember I've looked at Mama critically and disapprovingly. At any rate since she got engaged to Alfred. Before than my memories are vague. I don't remember much about Mama. Mostly it was Grandma, her mother. We lived with her. She was a widow too, and had a two-room apartment. Mama was busy sewing and fitting the whole day. She had to do something to support herself and me. My father didn't leave a penny and her mother's pension didn't stretch far.

So it was Grandma who looked after me. We went out shopping hand in hand, bought bread and milk in the street where we lived and groceries on the corner. Now and then we walked in the park and looked at the swans. At night before I went to sleep she read the evening prayer with me and made sure my ears were washed; she read aloud fairy tales—when I'd been really good. No, I don't remember much of Mama from that time. She swept through the room, hugged and kissed me so my hairbow fell off and my dress got crumpled, and then she was gone again. There was always so much confusion around her. It was secure with Grandma. And when she died, everything was different.

Even though her actual death didn't come as a blow. I couldn't have understood much about it. Anyway, I wasn't home then. I went to a boarding school when Grandma became ill, and I was gone the whole year. When I returned Alfred and Mama were married and I moved with them. Thinking about it now, Grandma's death was a catastrophe for me, a disaster, which put an end to my relatively happy childhood. But at the time it didn't seem so. It was more like an enormous emptiness that moved in on me gradually, something gray and oppressive, which sunk over me and weighed down my heart. It angered me that Mama could be so happy.

I remember how my annoyance throbbed up during puberty and burst into a yellow, feverish hatred. Everything about her got on my nerves: the well-rounded, white arms, the bleached hair, the red-lacquered nails, the ridiculously high heels, the red-tipped cigarette butts in the ashtrays—and not least the heavy, cloying perfume that was like a symbol of her stifling, luxurious life. It was enough to make me scream. . . .

But when the war came and forced her to get up early in the morning and to do her own housework, down to washing the floors, that irritated me just as much—perhaps even more. Her refusal to whine—not that she has ever whined; she has a certain sardonic humor that really emerged during the war. And that she took on a new character, as a "housewife," as a "good Norwegian patriot," admired and applauded by Alfred of course. It was her new and unexpected good qualities, the way she went around taking everything—the war, the lack of food, the Occupation—with "good humor." It was almost enough to make you side with the enemy. If they had been Nazis, she and Alfred, that would have been an incentive to be active in the underground. But they were "good patriots." Alfred, in fact, was imprisoned for several months. It was *their* war from the first, with the news from London on three times a day—Mama had a radio in the woodpile and read illegal newspapers—and the constant assurance, "England always wins one battle—the last one." I've never been able to understand this country's groveling worship of all things British. Of course I was anti-German—after the invation of Norway on April 9th. I wasn't a German sympathizer, that I was not. And if I'd been with Bente and Gro during the war . . . But of course I'd cut all ties, isolated myself completely. The only people I saw were Mama and Alfred and their friends. I was cool to their war—well, not cool, but lukewarm. And today they're still doing the right thing. Mrs. Bugge has been to Sweden three times for new clothes. The red-lacquered nails have reappeared, along with the perfume and the high-heeled shoes. She clatters around with an unabashed air, because during the Occupation she actually stood in line and washed the floors and trusted in England the whole time. Oh, there are many miles between us now.

But that last spring before the war we were actually—well, friends is probably too strong a word, but our relationship was at least friendly.

I remember a Sunday, a radiant Sunday towards the end of February. One of those shiny, silky blue days during the winter-spring, when the sky is dizzyingly high, when manure lies spread out in black heaps over the white fields, when tufts of grass are beginning to shoot up. And the air is astonishing, irresistible. You keep looking up into all that blueness, feeling oddly weak and happy. It was a Sunday like that.

Bente had gone skiing on the steely bright slopes of Nordmarka; she probably wouldn't come home until late. But Gro and I tramped the brown sodden roads out to Bygdøy, past the King's white summer home, lying stately and secluded behind black, wrought iron gates, past the bright red farmhouses where everything smelled of manure and stables. In the King's Forest we searched for blue anemones on brown, southerly hillsides. It was still too early. But Gro discovered pussy willows and long, dangling catkins that sprinkled gold dust over the thin carpet of snow.

I barely got back home again in time to change. The sun was low over the roofs when I stumbled through the streets in my slippery boots. It froze in the evening and it felt much colder. For the first time it gave me a sense of well-being to stand in the brightly lit hall and have my coat helped off. I looked forward to the thought of the large warm rooms with the polished floors and the deep easy chairs, to Mama clattering up with a "Hello, Edle!" and to Alfred waiting with the silver cocktail shaker, ready to pour our drinks, bitter and brown, into high-stemmed glasses.

My face must have reflected some of this cozy expectation or perhaps my cheeks were red from my walk, because I remember Mama cried out, "Edle, you're looking so well!"

And that didn't annoy me; on the contrary, it unleashed a feeling of spontaneous kindness.

"You've gotten thinner," I said.

"Do you really think so!"

She smoothed her hips, pleased and surprised, as if I'd arrived with roses. "Yes, I've lost a little weight this last week. Massage does wonders. But I didn't think that anyone else would notice it." (That you would notice it!)

And I thought to myself, It takes so little!

She seemed decidedly slimmer, whether that was due to the massage or to her dress, a black wool outfit with white trim, not tight-fitting and coquettish as usual, but simple, schoolgirlish, long-sleeved with white cuffs. She looked so young— she was, too, younger than her daughter, with a childlike appetite for pretty, expensive things, for all the good things in life.

Dinner itself was unusually pleasant. We had juicy red roast beef with peas and french-fried potatoes, and for dessert Pêche Melba in tall pink glasses. Alfred served his best red wine; he didn't say much, but sat there stout and good-natured. Mama kept up a flow of chatter, telling amusing anecdotes, asking about my classes, about Bente. And suddenly, without knowing quite how, I was in the middle of the story of little Harald's christening and the uproar in Lillevik. Mama thought it was "wildly funny!" (Imagine Edle telling something amusing for once!) and asked if I couldn't bring "Mrs. Arnesen" for dinner someday.

"I really haven't been able to say hello to her since she moved to Oslo," she complained. "You really keep your friends in wraps, Edle."

Of course, nothing came of it. Seen with ordinary and more sober eyes it was a stupid idea. Anyway, Mama went to the Skodsborg Spa right afterwards and then to the mountains with Alfred. But even if she'd been at home, there wouldn't have been much point in bringing Bente there. What would the two of them have in common? Mama is basically very conventional. And all those clothes and the perfume—Bente would have just gotten annoyed. But the mere fact that for a moment I believed it possible shows how conciliatory I was feeling.

We had coffee in the library, strong good coffee in the green demitasse cups. But the coffee tray was no longer, as in the old days, a secret signal to Edle to disappear upstairs. It was, on the contrary, an invitation to relax and enjoy myself.

When I was ready to leave, I shook both Mama's and Alfred's hand cordially and said, "Thank you so much. It's been lovely." I *was* thankful. I *had* had a nice time. And Mama invited me to come back again *soon*, while Alfred chuckled, "You know you're always welcome here."

But both Mama and I realized that the evening had been an exception. Perhaps we could meet in the same conciliatory mood occasionally, but not often—by no means often. Such impersonal goodwill couldn't be sustained for long. Sooner or later she'd feel obliged to nag me about my appearance—Why didn't I go have a really proper skin treatment? Why didn't I try a hair conditioner (It really helps against dandruff; you know dandruff and oily hair go together)—and I would look at her and gradually feel sickened by her perfumed elegance. No, it was best to keep my distance and just see her once in a while in a friendly way. But just the fact of that evening and our enjoyment in each other's company was a step forward. It made me feel good. And I wonder . . . though it's probably too late for that now too.

VI

Gʀᴏ ᴡᴀꜱ ᴛʜᴇ ᴏɴᴇ who brought Hans Jørgen over. She came tromping across the University square, large and radiant. Her curly mop was more unruly than ever. The tilted eyes laughed.

"Hi there, Edle!"

It was like a fanfare: Wake up and look around. All of a sudden I noticed how blue the sky was behind the thick, surging banks of clouds. How the smell of snow thawing and dripping was the smell of spring.

"Here I am with a protégé for you, someone who needs some advice about History." And she introduced Hans Jørgen.

He was a childhood friend of hers, the son of the judge in her hometown, who'd been living here for five or six years. He'd started out studying law, but had transferred over to Humanities and studied French. Then he'd toyed a little with journalism and done some work for various publishing houses. Now he wanted to go back to the University and get a regular degree. He was thinking of History as a major but wasn't quite sure.

Gro had run into him and pounced on his uncertainty. "I know someone who can help you." There was nothing out of the ordinary about it. But this first meeting came to appear to me as enormously meaningful. Gro became the goddess of Fate, striding over with Hans Jørgen in her outstretched hand: "Here I am with Life's gift to you!" Well, not then, when it actually happened . . . but later. At the time it was rather prosaic. I fidgeted, mumbling that I didn't know all that much about the History courses; I'd barely started to study it myself. And Gro complained, "Are you going to spoil everything! I've bragged so much about you! Don't believe her, Hans Jørgen, it's just false modesty. Edle is my conclusive argument, my concrete proof that women are truly capable of logical thinking."

"I know I have some nerve coming to sponge off you after I've just been going around in a daze," said Hans Jørgen with the charming, easy smile that was his trademark. "But it would be nice of you."

Of course, I'd help; I offered immediately to make up a schedule of lectures and a preliminary reading list for him. It wasn't any trouble at all—I'd enjoy it. If he'd like he could come with me to the seminar I was taking part in—the 1870s in Germany, the industrial-economic development under Bismarck.

The medical students wandered across the square in their white coats. The steps outside Domus Media were thickly covered with students, pallid from the reading room, waiting for the sun with upturned faces like wan house plants. Suddenly it appeared, streaming through a white bank of clouds, flooding the square with warm golden light, while the hungry, sallow faces turned sensual with enjoyment.

There I stood on the steps outside the psychology building with Gro and the unknown Hans Jørgen. And the whole world was full of yellow daffodils.

It was Hans Jørgen's description. "Look at this weather! It reminds me of masses of yellow daffodils." With his singularly lazy smile.

When he wasn't smiling he was nothing much to speak of. That struck me when I saw him at the movies the other day. It was the same in those days too. He was always a little smaller, a little skinnier, a little more colorless when you saw him than you had remembered.

At the moment it's almost impossible to recall how he actually looked. Smooth blond hair, light blue eyes placed closely together. But his face itself is an empty oval. His smile I remember, but not as an expression on his face, or a movement of his mouth—more the sensation of it, the effect it had, of comfortably loosening things, almost like alcohol.

"Now I've got to run," said Gro, and tromped up the steps. But something warm and restorative remained in the air. Even though the sun had vanished behind an armada of clouds that had sailed out of the deep blue sky, you felt it was there, kept feeling the warmth of its golden light.

Hans Jørgen went with me up to Auditorium Six for a lecture on the Crusades. The auditorium was packed; the heating stove glowed red. Through the tall windows we could see the royal palace and the blue sky.

I scribbled energetically and my sharp blue script ran across and down the pages. But the whole time I was feeling the presence of Hans Jørgen.

He sat quite still, with an attentive, listening profile. His hands lay on the desk, loosely folded, narrow, white. They looked like they didn't belong there. There was something meticulous, masculine about his light gray suit, his faint odor of shaving cologne. Once he raised his hand to his chin and cleared his throat slightly. He wasn't at all near me, but it felt as if he were touching me. I could, in fact, feel his hand on my breast.

Old maid fantasies. But it wasn't *that* foolish. I was young, just twenty-two, and ugly women get pregnant and even get married. Why shouldn't I be allowed to feel that way . . . Why shouldn't I be allowed to go to Hans Jørgen and say . . . Why not me as well as Kit . . . as well as everyone else.

A time came when Hans Jørgen almost displaced Gro. We attended the same lectures, had seats next to each other in the reading room. He had lunch together with me and Bente. But Bente didn't like Hans Jørgen.

"The lazy slug," she said. "He's weak through and through."

Later she glossed over it. "Even so, he can be a nice guy." As though she wanted to console me. Poor Edle—when she's finally found herself a boyfriend.

"Well, not everybody can be a sports star," I said bitingly. She looked at me in astonishment.

"That wasn't what I meant. It has nothing to do with sports. Don't be so stupid, Edle, a smart girl like you!"

Of course she hadn't meant it that way, and she *hadn't* been thinking "poor Edle," at any rate not until I gave her the idea. When I think about it now, I acted exactly like a fifteen-year-old who's gotten a crush for the first time and is making a big deal of it.

Poor Hans Jørgen had to be propped up, furnished and embellished with a number of qualities he completely lacked. As if that weren't enough, my feelings for Hans Jørgen also had to be built up and embellished until they came up to a conventional standard, until what could have been a fruitful friendship, a little something extra in my life, became something so artificial and inflated out of proportion that it lost all taste.

I quickly discovered that Hans Jørgen liked me and enjoyed my company. But that wasn't enough. I had to have him down to the last fingertip, put my stamp of ownership on him—preferably in the form of a shiny ring that could announce to the world that he was *mine—my* man.

I blush to see it on paper. But it's true—that's how it was. I felt that was the only way I could feel completely free. I had to have conventional proof that I was acceptable as a woman before I went my own way. I knew myself that marriage would never suit me. A house and home could never be the same to me as my studies were, as scholarship. I'd never be able to give up History, I thought at the time. (Strange, because that's exactly what I have done—betrayed my studies for this deadly teacher's job.) If marriage and my studies couldn't be reconciled, it was the home that would have to lose out. I knew that. But I didn't want to have "'the grapes are out of reach,' said the fox" thrown in my face. I didn't want anyone to think I couldn't have what any idiotic young girl thought she could get. *I wanted to be like everyone else.* And at the same time, I wanted to go my own way. No wonder I felt torn.

What did Hans Jørgen see in me? I suppose a man like him always needs a confidante, an intellectual woman friend he can talk to, someone who doesn't eternally parade her sex, but is, all the same, a woman, understanding, interested.

If it's true what Virginia Woolf says, that men need a woman as a mirror—see how big and clever I am compared to you—it wasn't like that with Hans Jørgen. He never tried to sparkle. In many ways he was quite modest, but he got along best with women. He reminded me a little of those refined, worldly young men who passed through the French salons of the seventeenth century, attentive cavaliers whose main duty it was to amuse and entertain the ladies in the "feminine century." He was amiability itself, witty, courteous and at bottom kind; he wouldn't hurt a fly. But he was weak, of course. Bente was quite right. Next to robust, sober men, who worked single-mindedly, determined to "make a go of it," he must have felt inferior; perhaps he felt secretly that he wasn't any good and had to turn to the "weaker sex" for confirmation of his manhood.

He was very musical, went to all the concerts and played the violin himself. Otherwise it was literature that he enjoyed most, especially poetry. He could get tears in his eyes over a poem by Verlaine. He was fond of reading aloud and often recited things in a slow, drawling voice. What he was doing taking History was something I could never fathom (even though I told myself that Hans Jørgen was brilliant and just needed to concentrate). It was probably a futile attempt to come down out of the clouds, but it didn't work out. He gave up the University that same spring and went back to journalism.

Poor Hans Jørgen. It can't be easy to be him in our sober, practical times—a poor butterfly who flits aimlessly around, just asking for a little sunshine. Harmless, loveable and totally useless, with a sense of doom lurking under the cheerfulness because he knows he's superfluous.

But at the time I saw him differently—a Werther, a Hamlet. And afterwards I trampled him down in cold disgust, because he hadn't lived up to my expectations.

74

What a good time we'd had together really, sitting side by side in the reading room, with Hans Jørgen so friendly, so thoughtful.

"Is there a draft on you, Edle? Won't you change places with me? Here's some fresh blotting paper for you."

He always had something to show me, to share with me—a story by Katherine Mansfield, an essay on Gide, a new poem that had caught his fancy.

"Have you read Rainer Maria Rilke? But you must. That man is a seer, a prophet, he sees right through things and into your very being. A unique sensibility."

And he got me to read *The Book of Hours*.

Days came when the sky whirled with snow. The city was snowbound, all noise smothered in soft white blankets, the mood that of *White Nights*. I always associate Dostoyevski with snow, for the same gently insubstantial atmosphere of light and dark. I sat by the window in the reading room and read *The Book of Hours*. It suited the picture of the snowy, muffled quiet in the street. But the poems left me quite unmoved; they were far too fervent and humble. Though when I talked to Hans Jørgen I feigned enthusiasm, not wanting my prosaic soul exposed.

But I once later came across another Rilke collection. It was in Hans Jørgen's room. He'd borrowed a studio apartment from a friend who was abroad, and I was there for coffee. The book lay on the table—I think it was called *New Poems*—and while Hans Jørgen made coffee in the kitchenette I picked it up and leafed through it.

There were some strange poems, one that I remember in particular, "Leichenwäsche." Three women washing a corpse. Painstakingly depicted in beautiful verse, as tender and reflective as his portrayals of "Rosenschale," and "Blaue Hortensia." There was another poem about a leper king, something about the disease breaking out and blooming like a flower on his forehead.

At first I didn't understand anything. I searched for meaning, for symbolism. Then it came to me—there was no deeper meaning. The hideous was portrayed for its own sake, praised

75

like a rose, a temple . . .

I can't explain it, but something happened—it strikes me now—it was like seeing the ocean, it was as if someone had taken the dirty blackened train station and planted it in the white snow of the University square and said, "Look, it's beautiful, because it's real." Involuntarily I thought of Gro, "You have to blossom, Edle."

"Hans Jørgen," I said, looking up from the book. "What a poem!"

He came in just then with the coffee tray and searched for a spot to put it. "Oh yes," he said absent-mindedly. "Horribly macabre, isn't it? Of course it's influenced by Baudelaire. Have you read 'Une charogne'? Quite appalling! A carcass swarming with maggots and flies, celebrated in magnificent lines of verse. Typical decadence."

I wanted to say something, but couldn't get it out. The impression I'd had had been so brief, so overwhelming, a flash of light, a sudden revelation. I hadn't quite absorbed it and now everything had faded. Typical decadence.

Afterwards we talked of other things and the poems were forgotten. How *could* I forget them, and so completely? To-morrow morning I'm going to the library to borrow Rilke's *New Poems* and perhaps Baudelaire as well . . .

Strange how things can disappear, to pop up again quite suddenly, as alive as if it were yesterday. I'd forgotten that incident. For such a long time the thought of Hans Jørgen has carried with it so much shame and aversion that the charm of that first stage of our friendship has evaporated. But now it washes over me again.

I was so preoccupied at the time with romanticizing Hans Jørgen and myself as well, that I never gave myself time to enjoy the actual intimacy and pleasure of the relationship. Why couldn't I have said what I felt: "To tell the truth, Hans Jørgen, *The Book of Hours* isn't for me. Religious mysticism leaves me cold. But these poems, Hans Jørgen—I'm completely taken by them, they've awakened something in me." Instead of suppressing a vision that could have meant so much, meant new perception, new growth. Just to please another person. Is it so certain that Hans Jørgen would have been disappointed? He had a great gift of empathy, a fine understanding of what was essentially different from himself—more than most men, I think. Perhaps it would have excited his interest, perhaps he could have made a discovery too. We could have discussed it and gone into it and Hans Jørgen could have helped me. He knew how to conduct an abstract intellectual discussion, if only he didn't have to put it into practice. Isn't that just what binds people together? Reciprocal openness and trust? How stupid I was. How idiotically stupid.

What was it my high school principal said to me at school? "You've been fiddling around so long with your personality, with what to make of your personality, that you've erased the whole thing." What have I done, my entire life, but erase and erase, until I've turned into zero, a nothing. The only thing I didn't erase was my self-conceit, my ego; that I've pampered and coddled, letting it eat into all I have of mental resources— and now it's all I have left, an ego wounded, curled up, like a maggot in a nut, the only thing remaining in the emptiness of the shell.

VII

THEN CAME THE DAY when Hans Jørgen asked me to go with him to the Humanities Society party. I'd had coffee at his place several times but had never been out with him before. It was an event.

A soft spring day at the end of March; the light so mild, sifting through a filter of golden-gray clouds, the air no longer piercingly sharp and giddy, but mild too, and gentle—caressing.

Everything about that day is alive for me, even though I haven't recalled it for years, have done everything *not* to recall it, have shoved it down haphazardly, packed it away like summer clothes in a chest and turned the key. I've kept it locked for eight whole years. Extraordinary that I can still take it out so entire, so unwrinkled—shake it out and have it fall in folds just as before. Even the fragrance is preserved, that faraway, thrilling fragrance of gentle spring light and sun-dried pavements.

We strolled across the University square, Hans Jørgen and I. The square itself was dry as a bone, but if you went around the corner to the student cellar your shoes got wet and muddy. It was darker on that side, with little sun. Here and there a dirty clump of snow lay next to the fence. But the birds chirped in the bushes and it felt as if there were a quiet hum in the air.

But why sit in the dark, overcrowded cellar where the smoke hovered so thickly that you could barely see each other? We preferred to eat outside. Bente wasn't with us. She had probably gone home for a book. It was just Hans Jørgen and me. We walked around carrying our lunch sacks, chewing and talking profoundly—about Dostoyevski, I believe. Hans Jørgen was going through a Russian period—reading Tolstoy, Goncharov, fantasizing about learning Russian. His History studies weren't going anywhere. I should have been nagging him perhaps, getting him to concentrate on the required reading, steering him down the narrow path. That was probably what Gro expected of me. But I only agreed obsequiously with what he said and let him hold forth on the Russians. That day in the square I was listening with half an ear, seeing myself from the outside, a tall thin girl in a dark-blue smock, a student like the others, who was walking with her male friend. And suddenly the chairman of the Humanities Society stood before us. I don't remember his name, but Hans Jørgen knew him. He knew everybody. A tall slim boy, very courteous.

"You two are coming tonight, aren't you?" he asked. "Of course you're coming. It's not every day that our Society gives a party." He kept talking, amiably persuasive, telling us about the large quantities of sausages and beer that had been ordered, about the dance band and about how many had already said they were coming. "Of course you two will be there!" He wouldn't listen to objections. And the whole time he said, "you two."

I wanted to sink into the ground, but at the same time I was hoping . . . What if Hans Jørgen answered, "But I don't have a girl to bring." The chairman would *look* at me and understand perfectly. The shame of it, the *shame*. Then what excuse could I give? Could I go with Bente, without an escort, sit like a wallflower while she danced—this was a party, after all, not an ordinary meeting . . . No, not for the world.

Hans Jørgen smiled his lazy smile, giving me a sidelong look, "What do you say, Edle? Do you think we should bother to go?"

It was like giving the right answer to a difficult exam question. I stood there short of breath, red in the face, not believing my good fortune. And I answered, "Y-yes, let's," in my driest voice.

"Okay, you can count us in," said Hans Jørgen. "But if it's

boring, we'll leave." (We—us!)

The breeze stroked my cheeks. I felt how soft it was. Heard the sleepy humming of everything that streamed and dripped behind us in the University garden. Took a deep breath and drew in the smell of wet black earth. It was as if something surged in me, burst open, so that tears almost came to my eyes. Even though I was just ugly, awkward Edle Henriksen, "who's so terribly intelligent, poor thing." No miracle had occurred, not to my nose or skin or hair. I as scrawny and gangly and pimply as before. It was just that I was going to a party. With a male friend.

But perhaps that meant I wasn't as impossible as I myself believed. Perhaps I'd made myself out to be worse than I was, turned myself into a caricature, after all my humiliations. Maybe it wasn't true that one's appearance was everything. And probably I could help myself a little. Go to the hairdresser, use powder, a bit of rouge or lipstick. For the first time I wished, really wished, that I had a new dress, something fresh and elegant, instead of my boring dark blue one.

Mama would have made a beeline for a fashionable store, choosing and discarding clothes, turning herself into a newly hatched butterfly. Clothes are her natural means of expression. But I'm different. Clothing has always been an effort for me, something to buy at regular intervals, because you have to, because that's the way it is. Because your mother wants you to and Alfred Bugge has enough money. "Of course you have to look nice, for Alfred's sake if nothing else. What would people say? About Alfred, who really is so kind and generous. . . ."

That's how I got my clothes. Mama went with me herself, steering me into salons where sales ladies came swarming like goldfish after breadcrumbs . . . "One moment, Madame, *just* one moment." Rolls of fabric were brought out, unfurled with a quick snap, draped over my shoulders . . . "Like this? Like that?" Mama studied me intensely, with narrowed eyes and her head to one side. It always had to be something subtle, something that disguised, that smoothed over. The sales ladies and seamstresses did all in their power to make my clothes unobtrusive enough. I just stood there, straight as a rod. Like a post.

But what if I were to go to Mama now and say, "I'm going out this evening. Will you help me find a dress?" She'd come flying, turning the fashion salons and sewing rooms upside down to get a dress knocked out. Perhaps not the red one I'd dreamed of, definitely not the red, but perhaps something in blue-gray or brown, a pretty new dress that would suit me. She'd be so delighted: "At last!" But that's a triumph I couldn't give her. It would have destroyed the defenses I'd built up through the years: that one's appearance meant nothing; that clothes were an affectation that was beneath me. It would have meant laying myself open so that she could march right in on her cruel high heels and do as she liked with me. "Because you must admit it yourself, darling, that I *am* right," and "Isn't this what I've always said?"

Besides, it was a ridiculous idea to buy a new dress in order to go to a Humanities sausage party. No doubt almost everyone would be wearing skirts and blouses. Even if it was the first time I'd been invited out by a young man what was there to celebrate? Just that what normal young girls took for granted was for me a big event.

I didn't buy a dress, but I went to the hairdresser before dinner and had my hair washed and set. And on the way to the place we always ate I went into a toiletry shop and bought an expensive American lipstick and a little bottle of perfume, *l'Heure bleue*.

For the first time since Bente had come to stay with me I was annoyed at her presence, at having to encounter her at dinner and meet the clear gaze that would take it all in and see, in deep distaste, that Edle had fixed herself up for a man. Edle!

I was right. At first she didn't say anything. She was already at the table when I arrived; she was occupied in choosing the first course and barely nodded to me. But then she came out with exactly what I'd expected. "Wow, you're so dolled-up. Did you go to the hairdresser's *today*? I thought you were going on Saturday?"

I'd prepared a long explanation about a misunderstanding, a

change of appointment. Strangely enough, she accepted it. At least she didn't say anything; she probably had other things on her mind. For suddenly, in the middle of her fish dinner, she burst out, "Sven's coming to Oslo tomorrow. I got a letter."

"Really," I answered, hearing how lame that sounded. If it had been six weeks ago I would have been feverish with uncertainty and fear and jealousy. Now I felt nothing. Only a stab of remorse at being so detached.

But Bente didn't seem to notice. She chewed her fish and kept furrowing her forehead the way she had in school when there was something in math she couldn't follow.

Then Gro tramped in, happy and out of breath as usual; she sank into a chair and began to take off her scarf, ulster, gloves, all at the same time.

"Umm, I'm so hungry! I haven't had a single bite since this morning. Is the cod any good? Or should I have fishballs?"

She planted her elbows on the table and looked from one of us to the other. "So, how's it going with you two? Edle's been to the hairdresser's, you can see that right away. You look really nice. You should always wear your hair like that, a little loose. It suits you . . . I hear you're going to the get-together tonight. I saw Hans Jørgen for a minute, so I know *all.*"

I bent over my plate and carefuly deboned my fish, placing the skeleton on the edge of the plate.

"Well, it was pure chance I went to the hairdresser's," I said. "My appointment was changed." What was the point, really? Why did I bother to lie?

"That was lucky," Gro said. "Since you're going out tonight and everything. Though I suppose you'd have changed your appointment anyway. It's so nice to get your hair done when you're going out," she continued. "You feel so much better."

I was a little embarrassed, but happy all the same. It was easy after all; it was natural.

It was a strange evening. Diffuse—I can't think of another word. Impressions, feelings, everything dissolving. There were no set contours, no precise boundaries, just a phantasmagoric jumble of talk and laughter, aimless and unclear, billowing here and there as if glimpsed through the plate glass wall of an aquarium.

I remember the sky, a clear transparent green, as we walked to the party; the crust of ice that cracked under our feet. Expectation like a polished diamond (nothing nauseous or diffuse about that). Hard and pure, it sparkled inside me.

But as soon as we came into the cloakroom, everything seemed to lose its shape. There were so many people, known and unknown. So much smoke and noise. There was no time to get a single clear impression. There seemed to be a fog surrounding everything and everyone. I couldn't make things out clearly. And my laughter bubbled up unceasingly, like a cough, impossible to stop. Because I'd been drinking, of course. Hans Jørgen had a flask in his pocket. Lots of people had flasks.

I remember I downed one gulp after another, "to get in the mood." To be equal to the confusion and laughter that rose like a flood around me. We sat at a long table that ran down the whole hall. Everyone sang. Me too, even though I've never kept a tune in my life. Sang and yelled and thumped my beer mug on the table. I shudder to think of it now. But I doubt anyone paid particular attention to me or what I did. They would have wondered more if I'd sat bolt upright in my chair, as stiffly correct as usual.

Odd the effect drinking could have. I was used to alcohol, after all. It was served in abundance at Alfred's parties. But generally I only got drowsy and heavy-headed. Never animated.

Yet at this party I was actually intoxicated. My inhibitions dropped off me like a loose wrap and I strutted proudly around in my nakedness. It's lucky the others were just as far gone.

I became completely uncritical. A feeling of goodwill washed over me; I could have embraced everyone. It was the first and last time I've had that Beethoven's Ninth Symphony sort of emotion. I was at one with the whole brawling, boisterous gathering, and at the same time I was supremely indifferent to what anyone said or did.

I can see Hans Jørgen's face. Red and smiling it swims before my eyes, close to me. The lips move; I hear the words without taking in their meaning. Just now they don't interest me. I'm enclosed in my own intoxication. But I feel his body, the knee that presses against mine. I recognize a shivery, stirring in my groin and knees.

Yes. I remember that. Clearly. Surely it must be proof of my sexual normality that I could feel this purely physical attraction to a man. Even if it was only once. I remember that afterwards I longed to feel it again. But I never did.

We must have sat at the table for hours. There were endless songs and speeches and toasts. At last people got up, somewhat unsteadily. And the dancing began.

That was what I'd been dreading. I'm a clumsy dancer, stiff and awkward, always out of step. But you could hardly say I've had any training. The dance parties I've been invited to I could count on one hand and I've usually sat them out. There was dancing with Alfred and his friends at the big parties at home. Excruciating dances of duty. Dancing has always been an agony to me, a demonstration of my ungainly clumsiness, always connected with the thought that someone is mandatorily sacrificing himself. I get stiff as a ruler, stumbling and striving in vain to follow along.

I'd thought of an excuse beforehand. I'd say that I'd gotten a blister and would suggest we sit and talk instead. Yet when the music finally started, I was seized with an uncontrollable *desire* to dance. I can't explain it. The desire was just there. It pushed its way through everything that was dissolving and groped with blind tendrils: the desire to dance, to feel Hans Jørgen's arms tight around me, the longing for a still closer physical contact.

The music beat out a quick step, and the floor immediately filled. People stamped, stumbled, clung to each other. Glistening red faces swayed around us; feet shuffled, tramped; the music screeched and soared. I have an intense memory of Hans Jørgen's cheek pressing against mine and the tingling faintness that ran through me. Then everything went under, sucked into a whirlpool.

One impression detaches itself from the mist. We stood outside in the hall; we'd probably gone out to get a little air—the atmosphere inside was terrible. I felt things clear a little around me and the air was cool on my forehead and cheeks. Hans Jørgen had his arm around my waist and we stood there swaying. Suddenly I felt his lips on mine, warm, soft. It didn't come as any surprise—this was the way it should be. I kissed him back, at length and with deep satisfaction. But whether it was the erotic experience that satisfied me or what it meant on a purely psychological level—the guarantee of my new worth as a woman—I can't say. It was all too vague and insubstantial. Someone laughed and pointed, "Hey, look at those two!" But not in surprise or scorn. It was vague too, a little silly, the way dreams are, when you accept everything and the next morning you wake up heavy-headed and the whole night's fantastic sights are gone and forgotten.

I wasn't ashamed either, even though now I wince at the very thought. I was proud. Proud! Proud and happy.

Oh, it's enough to make you sick. Crumbs, crumbs, crumbs! Being content with so little. Me, Edle Henriksen, who is so incredibly talented, "someone equipped with rare gifts," as our old principal said so beautifully. Experiencing my greatest happiness at a Humanities Society beer party, among half-drunk students. A peak experience that consisted of a completely ordinary young man (the type who never succeeds at anything) condescending to kiss me.

The next morning when I woke up, with a thundering headache naturally, the feeling of happiness was still there. Like a light inside me. Because the slightly drunken Hans Jørgen had kissed me. Because a man had lowered himself to take erotic notice of me—or, more exactly, of a hazy female who happened to be there.

VIII

BY MORNING WINTER HAD RETURNED. The room was freezing, the floor ice cold. Pale gray daylight grimaced from the window. Outside, small hard granules of snow flew by. As I said, I had a headache and an unpleasant taste in my mouth. I loathed the thought of Heckscher's economic history, loathed the thought of studying at all.

Yet there was a certain cozy quality to the pale, snow-lit morning. Bente was up already and doing exercises on the floor. I remained lying on my side and looked at her. The quick, supple bend-stretch-extend-extend looked invigorating. I felt tempted to bound out of bed and start myself. If my head hadn't ached so . . . But I enjoyed just lying there looking. Everything was in some odd way right this morning— just the way it should be. Not rough and prickly as it so often was, but smooth and harmonious. I stretched and yawned luxuriously. If I didn't study for one day, what did it matter? Tomorrow I'd be more in the mood than ever, I felt. Today I could take it easy.

But I wanted to go to the reading room—to see Hans Jørgen. And not just him. I wanted to see the others too, everyone I'd laughed and sung with yesterday, everyone who'd seen me dance with Hans Jørgen. I suddenly felt I belonged in the reading room and looked forward to going there.

"Was it fun last night?" Bente asked me on her way to the bathroom.

I wanted to tell her about it, to relive that giddy sense of being let loose. But the water was already spurting in the shower, and Bente was spashing around under it. I would have had to shout to be heard. And what words could I fix on? How was it possible to communicate? I had lots of fun. I really enjoyed myself. Empty, dry words that said nothing.

Bente appeared in the doorway wearing a red robe, with a brush in her hand.

"Edle?" She leaned forward slightly with her head to one side and brushed with long strokes. The dark mane crackled. "Edle, do you have anything against me bringing him home—here, I mean—this evening? After we've eaten. It's so exasperating to sit in a restaurant when you're really trying to talk."

Who? What was she talking about? Of course, Sven, her husband. He was supposed to arrive today, and I'd totally forgotten. My face grew warm; I felt embarrassed, and guilty as well. How preoccupied with myself I'd been. Though Bente was self-absorbed, too. Throwing me a dutiful, "Was it fun last night?" and then disappearing into the bathroom without waiting for an answer. All the same my guilty conscience continued to prick me.

"Yes, of course," I stammered. "I can go take a walk so you won't be disturbed. I can go visit Gro or Hans Jørgen."

As I said it, the thought flared up in me that I really could do that. Invite myself over to Hans Jørgen's. "You know, I don't have anyplace to go this evening." That was true, after all. And he'd smile heartily, "Sure, come on over."

But Bente shook her head, brushing energetically. "To tell the truth ... I'd really like ... for you to come along." She straightened up. "Then we could come here and have coffee afterwards. I can go out and get some Danish pastry."

I remember that it struck me: I should be proud and happy. But I wasn't. I could have had coffee at Hans Jørgen's; instead I was going to be a buffer, taking the blows between the two of them. And it was Sven who was in the right. I was realizing just how in the right he was. Bente was childish, immature, an untamed filly who couldn't bear to be harnessed. I was going to have to take her part and support her against my better judgement.

"I can promise you that there won't be a scene," said Bente quickly. "There's never a scene when Sven is around."

"Naturally. Of course. If you really *want* me to."

I heard myself how unenthusiastic that sounded and immediately repented. Because Bente might pull back now, toss her head and answer, Thanks, but I'm not going to beg you! Proud, arrogant Bente.

But she didn't. "I need moral support," she said, with a little laugh, and she brushed her hair so sparks flew.

Hans Jørgen wasn't in the reading room, and he never arrived. The door opened and closed and each time I gave a start it was always someone who didn't matter. Most likely he was sitting peacefully at home, nursing his headache and reading his beloved poetry.

It annoyed me. I couldn't calm down enough to read because I was so irritated. If I could sit here reading the history of economics, he could damn well drag himself down here too. He was the one who really needed to study, I thought bitterly, and immediately regretted it. It was one of the facts that had to be constantly squashed down and prettied up—that I was intellectually superior to Hans Jørgen. It didn't fit with the stereotype of a romantic relationship, where the man is big and strong and clever and protects his weak little woman. It was better in the end to sit here thinking sadly that Hans Jørgen was more concerned with his aching head than with any longing to see me. Strangely enough, it was less painful a thought.

I didn't see anything of the happy people from the night before either. There were unusually few faces I recognized in the reading room that day. But it was full, without a single empty seat and there was an unusually dismal, neutral air about the place—like shallow water. Only after I'd been sitting there over an hour did I discover that the chairman of the Humanities Society sat across from me, but he was so deep in his studies that he neither saw nor heard.

Gro was at the Blindern campus and Bente in town. I ate lunch alone in the student cellar with my nose in a book, almost like before. And then I shuffled back to the reading room.

Oh, the crushing stillness of that reading room. Everyone sitting packed together, head in hands, brow furrowed—the very air was oppressive. And it was never *quite* still. There was always someone clearing his or her throat, rustling, breathing heavily, moving around in the chair, or padding across the room to bend over someone else's shoulder, talking in a whisper. Those who sat nearby pulled their shoulders together slightly, hunched over their books and waited, with suppressed hostility, for the whispering to stop; the hissing whispers cut the quiet like saw blades.

Hans Jørgen talked about it once. "Isn't it odd? Here we sit, side by side, close together, all of us in different worlds. Someone's in Italy, wandering around in ancient Rome, standing in the Roman Forum swathed in a toga, listening to Caesar orate. Someone else is drinking champagne with Russian Grand Dukes, tossing glasses against the wall, throwing himself into his troika and driving in icy haste through the winter night, or loitering in solitude along the banks of the Neva. Someone's attending a ball in the Tuileries; someone else a masquerade ball in Venice; maybe someone else is standing on Denmark's desolate coast and spouting melancholy philosophy with a skull in his hand. So many different ways of life. So many colorful moods in this dreary room. Isn't it odd?"

Yes, it was odd. You wouldn't believe it to look at them. Heavy, closed faces. Yawns and groans. They didn't look as if they were investigating the fantasy worlds of either St. Petersburg or Venice. You wouldn't believe they were youthful explorers digging into the riches of world literature. They experienced nothing. They kept grinding away, struggling with the subject. Patiently, laboriously, unsmilingly. Through the window the sky was a uniform shade of gray and snowflakes flew sparsely through the biting wind.

It was a relief when it finally got so late that I could gather up my books and notes and shut them up in my locker with a hostile slam. There weren't many people left in the reading room. The chairs gaped emptily. Only books still lay there, like deserted, untidy islands on the long tables, evidence that their owners would come back to continue the never-ending cramming throughout the afternoon.

Someone opened a window and a gust of cold gray air blew in. It was good to get out of there. And after such a long and insignificant day there was something exciting about the thought of seeing Bente and her husband.

Sven looked older and more manly than I'd expected. A blond, handsome fellow with a decided mouth and chin—blue eyes, I think, or maybe gray; not very tall, but straight-backed and wide-shouldered. I remember the little start I gave when I saw him: Bente's Sven was so good-looking. And then my annoyed thought: Imagine having everything and running away from it! Yes, I was actually annoyed with Bente. I need-ed a kind of release after my long gloomy day; I broke out in unreasonable irritation at Bente.

The atmosphere was rather forced, naturally enough. Bente was silent and sullen and I had the uncomfortable sense of being an outsider, yet at the same time much too involved. Sven must have been wishing me far far away. Yet, of the three of us, Sven seemed the most unflappable. He chatted about this and that and, when he only got sulky monosyllabic replies from Bente, he turned to me and talked as amiably and unaffectedly as if we'd been old friends.

I've always had a great deal of admiration for people who can master a situation. When someone is obviously taking pains to maintain appearances in company you can't very well sabotage it and just sit there like a bump on a log. But Bente could. And I thought of her childlike triumph when she bap-tized the boy Harald and of Sven going around with a smile, smoothing things over. How could she be so childish!

Sven talked a lot about his son; he told us how big he'd gotten and how many teeth he had and that he could sit or stand or whatever a child of eleven months does. Gro should have been there. But not for a minute did he give the impres-sion that he blamed Bente for leaving or that he was trying to lure her back. It was as if it were the most natural thing in the world that she was here and he was in Lillevik with the baby. Yes, eventually everything seemed so natural that you felt quite embarrassed, for worrying so much about it and making too much of a situation that was simple and straightforward. So I thought. And suddenly, without warning, I was caught off-guard by an intense pity for Bente.

The sunken dark head, the immobile face, with the profile of a classical Greek woman; she sat staring at her plate and there was something about her, something helpless, maybe even touching, since I could feel such an absurd pity—I who was at bottom angry with her for catching me up in her childish pranks.

At one point she lifted her head and looked stiffly at him and said, as if she wanted to completely do away with me (after making me come here), "Sven, there's something I have to say to you."

But before she was able to continue, Sven had waved to the waiter and asked for the bill.

"We'll wait until later for that," he said calmly. And Bente bit her lower lip, but said nothing.

All the way home I shivered and froze, not because it was cold—it had already gotten a lot milder, with a warm thawing wind, and there was a pale blue sky peeking through the misty cloud cover—but because I dreaded, dreaded intensely the scene that Bente was building up to. I saw by looking at her that there was a storm in the works. As soon as we came in the door it would break loose. But I got off cheaply.

"Bente," said Sven, "The two of us have a lot to talk about, as I'm sure you'll agree. But I think we should spare Edle our private conversation. What about a cup of coffee now, all three of us?" he suggested, turning to me, "And then I'll steal Bente for a bit; we can have a stroll and talk things over. Afterwards I'll be off."

I was already in the midst of a stammering explanation: I'd been intending to leave so that the two of them could talk undisturbed, but Bente hadn't wanted me to.

I thought I'd noticed something disapproving in his tone when he said that about sparing Edle our *private* conversation. I was so afraid he'd think I was a parasite who lived off other people's intimate lives, that that was what I sustained myself on. I was, everything considered, afraid—afraid and abject.

"Sven," said Bente stiffly. "Edle is my friend. I asked her to be here and she promised me.

"You promised me," she said accusingly.

I squirmed miserably.

"Bente," said Sven, with a smile in his voice. "I didn't think you were such a coward."

That decided it. Bente turned red and answered vehemently, "All right then, if that's how you want it! Just go ahead, Edle!"

I slunk out with my tail between my legs, like a dog being quarreled over. Bente would have rather had me there, but then they'd agreed to let me go anyway.

Why didn't I say anything? Why didn't I stay and take Bente's side? I don't understand it—me, who'd dreamed of the moment when I'd stand up and fight for her, show that I was a real pal.

Was it because Sven was so different than I'd expected, not at all tyrannical and bourgeois, but common sense itself, amiable and tolerant? You had, albeit unwillingly, to agree with him. Maybe it was mixed up, in some deep and inexplicable way, with my feelings for Gro and Hans Jørgen, with my new self.

I don't know. I only know that I betrayed Bente that day, betrayed her shabbily and shamefully. I understand that now. Not that it hurt Bente. But you can't betray someone else without betraying yourself.

I went over to Gro's. She was at home. We sat on the bed with the patchwork quilt and talked intimately. Not about Bente and the scene that was even now taking place in my studio; I didn't mention it, out of loyalty to Bente I imagined. It was the Humanities Society party we talked about. The memory effervesced again, suplanting Bente and Sven. The dismal day at the reading room parted like a curtain to let the evening's festivities shine forth.

I might have said something about the red dress I'd wanted to have. For Gro said, "Why don't you buy yourself a bright red outfit, Edle? It'll put some color in your cheeks—brace you up. A bright red suit to celebrate spring in."

Which meant she understood.

By the time I came home Sven had gone. He'd taken the evening train back to Lillevik, Bente informed me. She sat reading with her legs slung over the arms of the chair; she almost didn't look up.

She's angry with me, I thought unhappily, angry and disappointed. Why didn't I stay and help her—if I could have been any help—instead of running away. It was as if I'd knocked over a costly vase, as if something valuable and beautiful had gone to pieces because of my clumsiness, and there I stood with the shards, not knowing what to do with them.

I can't be the only one to feel like this. There must be others who are clumsy and awkward when it comes to fragile situations. Maybe most people are. In the theater and in literature everything is so solidly and logically built up. Dialogue and plot are always significant, pointing in a single direction and illuminating people's characters in incisive flashes. But reality...? A meaningless hodge-podge of irrelevant, unimportant details. You stumble around, say all kinds of random things, hackneyed and conventional, with a little truth mixed in. But the tiny pearls drown in an ocean of triviality. The overall impression is one of disorder and nothing is clear. What about our precious individuality that we hold in such great esteem? It's just a pile of impressions, our own and others, shoved together aimlessly and accidentally.

Perhaps Bente was feeling something similar and it made her forgiving. At any rate she wasn't angry. Her voice sounded apologetic and a little embarrassed when she finally spoke.

"You probably think I'm one big failure, Edle. Boasting like a hero, but a coward under fire. Isn't that how it goes? But anyway, I'm going home."

She was silent. I tried to say something; I wanted to pretend surprise, but failed utterly. I'd known it all along.

Bente wasn't listening to me anyway. She sat kicking her legs against the chair, talking to the air.

"Oh yes, I'm going home. To Lillevik. And all my big words about education and backbone and independence, that's all just empty talk. Because when it comes down to it, I can't manage to go through with it. After you've put your head in the trap it doesn't help to complain that you want to be set free. You made your bed and can lie in it, and that's the truth. And besides, I wouldn't get anywhere anyway. All I'm good for is making trouble."

I protested lamely.

"No Edle, I'm just a big bag of hot air. But done is done and all you can do is make the best of it. I can't very well wreck Sven's life too."

She was silent again. I imagined Sven in the room, kneeling on the rug. "Bente, do you want to destroy my life?" Odd. One minute a person could sit talking over the table in a restaurant; the next he was getting down on his knees, begging for happiness. That was a silly thought, of course. Sven wasn't the sort to go down on his knees.

"You see," Bente said. "Sven wanted a direct answer. He understood that I needed freedom, that I needed to educate myself and be someone on my own. He understood all that." She swallowed. "But he didn't want to wait and wait in suspense—reasonably enough. He wanted it to be either/or. Either I had to come home right away and everything had to be like before, or else we'd get a divorce. And then he'd have to let me have the boy."

She bent over and plucked at a stockinged leg, scraping off a little speck, a mud splash perhaps.

"He loves the boy," she mumbled indistinctly. "I think I told you that. But that's exactly why he wants the boy to stay with me. He believes that the right thing, the important thing is that a little kid is with his mother. I told him," Bente said in a shaking voice, "I told him that I was sure he'd be ten times better at bringing him up than me—the way I am now, anyway. And he'd have his mother and sister and the whole family to help him. But he felt that his mother wasn't fit to bring up kids, she coddled them too much and so on. Well, of course, I know that . . . And he wants Harald to be a regular boy and be like me." She smiled crookedly. "So now I'm going back to make the best of it."

I was dumb with admiration at Sven's cleverness. Bente who'd dreamed of going back to fetch her son forcibly, of carrying him away out from under their noses, in spite of entreaties and protests. To get him just like that: Here you are, if you've got the nerve, just take him. How crafty. How vile.

But why hadn't Bente seen through it, why was she letting herself be lured back into the cage? Bente who hated cheating and half measures and conventionality. How could she be so gullible, so easy to steer, sharpsighted, indomitable Bente? I smiled inwardly. It was a relief to be able to see Bente as a capricious child who didn't really know what she wanted. At the moment I preferred to see her that way, rather than as an adult, with a grown woman's problems.

But now I wonder . . . her voice sounded so tired, disappointed and tired, I remember that now. It was just that I closed my ears to it then. I didn't want her to be disappointed—in me. But she was. And not just in me—I was only a part of it. She was disappointed in everything, sorry and disappointed, because it had to be that way. In the end she *had* no other choice.

"It will be a little different though," said Bente pensively, as if she were examining an old garment to see what could be made of it. "Sven thinks we could manage without a nanny. He thinks it would be better if I took care of the boy myself. And we're going to move. Sven has gotten a house outside Lillevik, a fair distance away, so we'll be on our own more. He said he understood that Lillevik got too confining for me."

"But then you've gained *something*," I said, with forced cheerfulness.

She didn't answer me right away; she just looked at me.

"Yes, maybe," she said lightly and gave a protracted yawn, stretching her arms above her head. "Well, now I'm going to bed. I'm worn out."

And I was grateful.

But I remember her look and it stings me now. That good-natured contempt: "Poor Edle, she barely understands anything at all. It's no use confiding in her anymore." I must have felt a little like that too at the time. But I shoved the feeling away.

95

IX

It was just after Sven's visit that Kit turned up. Bente hadn't left yet anyway. She'd decided to stay until Easter. Yet she made no secret of the fact that she was returning to Lillevik and seemed quite pleased. You wouldn't have believed she was making a sacrifice.

She talked constantly about her little son. She'd almost never mentioned him before. Now he was the one she was going back to; he was the central figure in the drama. Curious, this sudden change; rather tiresome in the end—everything the two were going to do together, when he just "gets old enough."

She was showing us photographs of the boy that Sven had brought her; it was lunchtime and we stood in the University square where it smelled of sun-drenched stone and hardened slush, a warm, springtime smell. Gro hung over Bente's shoulder and devoured each new photo with her eyes.

"Oh Bente, he's so sweet! Oh Bente, so cute!"

I felt a complete outsider. To be honest, all infants look alike to me and I've never been able to understand this gushing enthusiasm for other people's babies. My standard compliments seemed like dry paper flowers next to Gro's fresh, living roses. That was the moment Kit suddenly descended upon us. She stood there smiling, bareheaded, in a light gray spring suit; her chestnut brown hair gleamed in the sun.

I hadn't seen her for ages, not since graduation, I think. But she was just the same, a thin little thing, sharp, freckled, with an untidy mane of shoulder-length, curly hair.

I had a caustic memory of her from high school: the class "enfant terrible"—an impertinent little character who snickered and said unpleasant truths. But I'd forgotten her charm, how captivating she could be when she wanted.

"But how *lovely* to meet you! How *are* you? Goodness, I never suspected that *you* were a student here, Bente! How fun!"

And so on in the same vein, until Bente interrupted her with a sullen, "This is Kit Westman, Gro, a girl who went to high school with us. And this is Gro Holme."

A girl who went to high school with us! And in that tone of voice! Even though I hated and feared Kit—how many times had I squirmed at her "wisecracks," terrified of what she might say next—I could never have brought myself to cut her off in that way, when she was trying to be so charming. You needed a Bente for that.

But Kit just snickered indulgently. "God, Bente, you haven't changed one bit!"

Bente grimaced, but didn't say anything. Kit paused, humming faintly to herself with her hands in her jacket pockets. Then she turned to me. "Edle! How *are* you? It's been *such* a long time."

Silly goose that I was, I tried to answer pleasantly—and with that Kit became part of the circle. After that it wasn't more than a few minutes before she began to tell us how *she* was, what madly exciting and amusing things *she'd* been doing. What hadn't she done during her six months in England, with weekends on great estates, debutante balls in London, Ascot, Aldershot and Oxford? I cursed myself because I couldn't keep envy off my face. I felt it creeping out and fastening itself hungrily around my mouth. Naturally that goaded her to make new claims. I knew they were all true—with certain modifications, but for the most part true. She has always known how to indulge herself. She takes what she wants, people, situations; she squeezes them all to the last drop. She always makes me think of the white ape in the "Forsythe Saga." She's like a little ape, Kit, clever and calculating, quick to point a finger and to laugh shrilly.

That laughter, that dry snicker; I can hear it now, at this moment.

In the autumn she was going to Paris. "I can't wait to be there!" She'd already begun to study French and wanted to attend some language classes at the University. "But goodness, I feel so small and stupid among all these madly learned people here," said Kit, and suddenly she became endearingly young and childlike.

I can't think of anyone less childlike than Kit. Everything she does is studied. I believe she was born an adult.

"Well, I'm going home for good to husband and child at Easter," said Bente. "So you'll have to force your company on Edle."

It was just what Kit deserved. She needed squelching. All the same I did everything to save the situation for her and to smooth over Bente's crassness. Promised to keep a lookout for her on the square and to eat with her now and then. And Kit was *so* grateful. "You're a darling, Edle. So *lovely* to see you again." She had to run, *unfortunately*, because she had a class. Of course they called them lectures here. And then she had to go to the dressmaker's and try on a new suit. She waved cheerfully and dashed across the square. I remember her legs in pale silk stockings. She's always had unusually slender, well-shaped legs.

"Well, well," said Gro, and looked from Bente to me with laughter in her eyes. She hadn't opened her mouth while Kit stood there.

"I can't stand that girl," said Bente savagely.

"That was fairly evident from the conversation," smiled Gro. "Yes, I see she could be a little tiresome in the long run."

"Not just in the long run," said Bente shortly. "And why in hell did you give the devil an inch, Edle? Even more than an inch. She'll end up eating you alive. How can you stand to deal with her!"

I reddened and mumbled something about politeness; you couldn't be out and out rude to a person.

"Politeness! Who gives a damn!" snorted Bente. "I'm

damned glad I don't suffer from that refined sensibility. I think it's more honest to speak out when you can't stand someone than to butter them up."

"I don't think Kit is so horrible," I said stiffly. "She can be both sweet and funny."

"Oh well, then," said Bente. "Suit yourself. Now I'd better get going, if I'm going to get anything done today. This good-for-nothing has been standing here talking her head off for an hour."

"Do you have time to come with me to the bookstore?" asked Gro, and linked her arm in mine. "There's a book they've promised to get for me. I hope it's come."

Arm in arm we sauntered down Karl Johan Street, bare-headed, with our coats hanging loosely over our shoulders. The sun shone. Young people stood talking in groups. A few walked by chattering to each other in elegant spring suits. It felt so easy to walk on the sunbaked sidewalk. Even Gro had taken off her rubber boots and wore low-heeled shoes. A tall man without a hat strolled by; his face was copper-brown above his bright white collar. People turned to look at him, but he strolled unconcernedly on, like a Greek god come down from Olympus.

From somewhere a car horn tooted long and persistently; it had probably gotten stuck. High above us an airplane buzzed.

"What do you think of her?" I asked. The question was eating at me.

"Well . . . I've only just met her," she said, "but it seems to me that she's a little pushy. Maybe she's better one on one."

"She makes me think of those old-fashioned little shops," she continued after a moment. "The ones that have everything between heaven and earth and put every scrap in the window. Like it's important to display all they have."

"Oh there's more to Kit than you saw," I said bitterly. "She's intelligent too, really intelligent and clever and . . ."

"Umm," said Gro. "I believe you. But nothing very unique. Or else that would have been put in the window too."

It was like a tooth that suddenly stops hurting. Of course. Kit *was* nothing. All facade and play-acting for the public.

Nothing to worry about. It was just at school, when I'd been childish and much too sensitive that she'd been able to wound me. But now I'd gotten away from all that, had become a grown-up self-sufficient person. Liberated. I had my own circle, my own world where I was somebody and Kit was nobody. Kit and her world meant nothing to me.

I accompanied Gro to the subway and then went slowly and reluctantly back to the reading room.

It was one of those intense spring days when the sunlight seems to suck all energy out of the body. Everything seemed colorless and insubstantial under the intense blue sky. I felt incredibly, voluptuously tired, could barely move my feet. The cloakroom at Domus Media was dark and cold as a funeral chapel. I dragged myself up the stairs and collapsed into an empty seat near the door, set my books on the table and leafed through them listlessly. My seat was actually in the side room, but I didn't bother to go in there; mostly I felt like putting my head on my arms and sleeping.

The window shade was pulled halfway down and under it the sun flowed in a broad stream over my open book, as if it were burning the paper. Someone got up quietly and crossed the drowsy subdued room with soft squeaky steps. I felt a hand on my shoulder, turned abruptly and looked up into Hans Jørgen's smiling face.

I'd been looking forward so intensely to meeting him again, but the expectation had effervesced too long in the glass and had turned flat and stale. I had both seen him and not seen him. Had greeted him on the square, had talked briefly with him at a couple of lectures. It felt like an eternity since that evening at the party, even though it probably hadn't been much more than a week.

I looked up at him. He smiled at me. But the sunshine outside, the light, the air, had made me so weak I didn't have the strength to feel anything.

"Edle," he said. "Come and have coffee at my place this afternoon. I really need to talk to a sensible person. And you're so damned understanding."

At the moment I was quite indifferent; I only nodded and

said I'd like to come. But later, on the way home, I made a mountain of the poor crumbs—"sensible," "understanding"—it was incredible what I made out of them. I only listened with half an ear to Bente, though she wasn't saying much either. Finally we walked in silence, preoccupied, and I thought about Hans Jørgen, Hans Jørgen who needed me. I was going to help and console him, prop up his self-esteem any way I could. Which was exactly what he wanted.

That was apparent when I arrived. It was a light, mild spring evening with longing in the air, and I was as full of expectation and sentimental heart-throbbings as any ladies' magazine heroine. I was wearing my new red suit, even though it was far too early in the year to be going around in a spring outfit in the evening; I ended up in fact with a red nose and head cold the next day. But I felt in high spirits, revived; I had fiddled with my hair for half an hour in the bathroom while Bente read the paper, had powdered over the worst pimples and doused myself with *l'Heure bleue*. Most likely I looked like a well-groomed scarecrow. But I remember I felt—yes, actually—pretty.

Hans Jørgen lit up when he saw me, stretching out both hands to pull me into his apartment. I imagined that his voice sounded warmer than usual. Perhaps it was too. But it was probably because he was greeting his soul-mother, his sensible, understanding friend. Clearly he was eager to pour out his feelings. He was so full of spleen and self-pity that it splashed over.

"Edle," he began, almost before we'd seated ourselves. "If you knew how I despise myself! Have you ever felt like you wished you could escape from your own loathsome self?"

Had I ever! I almost had to laugh. He'd certainly come to the right person. But it wasn't me he wanted to talk about, I knew that for a fact, so I only nodded understandingly and said nothing.

We drank coffee in an atmosphere of brooding melancholy, with a dash of *fin de siècle* and *de profundis*.

"Maybe you think I don't realize it myself," said Hans

Jørgen with a wavering smile, "But in spite of everything I have a kernel of self-criticism intact and I'm quite aware, at least during the times I have the courage to face it, that I'll never amount to anything."

Odd—but it strikes me now that it was true. It *was* true. He did know that he'd never amount to anything. And this was one of the few moments when he had the courage to see it. It was one of those hard, naked moments that *can* be the starting point of something new. When you're down to rock bottom and finally have something firm to build on.

It's doubtful, of course, that Hans Jørgen had enough backbone to grab hold and really build anything from the bottom up—highly doubtful. Though Gro certainly believed he could. Gro had, in fact, the small faith in Hans Jørgen that I lacked. And now she wanted me to . . .

Strange, but it's suddenly occurred to me—incredible but obvious all the same—that it was me who betrayed Hans Jørgen. Not he who betrayed me. I betrayed him that evening, deliberately betrayed him while watching out for my own interests.

I can see him before me. He sits fiddling with his cigarette lighter, his gaze flickers, searching for a fixed point, while his face, like a child's, is helpless and imploring. . . . He implored me so sincerely that day; he beseeched me on his knees for one little straw of reality, something to cling to, to raise himself up to. And I handed him a new fantasy.

What if I'd opened up to him: "Oh, I understand so well, Hans Jørgen, because I feel exactly the same. You mustn't believe that you're the only one who doesn't measure up. What am I good for? All my splendid exams are merely a thin floor over a gaping cellar. You have so much that I don't, far more than I, when it comes down to it. Both of us need to begin at the bottom, to build a structure that's low and secure and to try to put down roots into the real world."

But I was so absorbed in my role as confidante, in polishing up my imaginary Hans Jørgen. I didn't want to see him as he really was, didn't want to expose a single one of my own secret wounds. Wasn't that the best way to win a man? Flatter him carefully and cleverly, lull him with false dreams, fan his vanity.

And it worked. Bit by bit he slipped back into his usual state of sentimental carelessness. He let himself be talked into reading Verlaine to me. Later he turned on the radio. We sat on the blue sofa and listened to a Chopin concert, and Hans Jørgen put his arm casually around my shoulders.

"I really like your perfume," he said.

"Oh? Yes, it's nice, isn't it? It's *l'Heure bleue*."

"*L'Heure bleue*," he caressed the words. "What a lovely name." And he kissed me lightly on the cheek.

So I was the one who reaped the benefits of that evening. . . .

There was cold clear moonlight in the streets when Hans Jørgen walked me home. But I shivered so much in my thin suit that I couldn't manage to talk.

"Thank you for the lovely evening, Edle," he said when we parted at the street door. "You don't know how much you've helped me. I was really down. And now I'm feeling on top again."

"Listen, you're going to get pneumonia," said Bente when I came in. "You must be completely crazy, girl. In that thin suit."

And then suddenly, with no transition, she said, "I'm telling you, Edle, you'll be a real fool if you settle for Hans Jørgen. He's never going to get anywhere. He'll only be a chain on your leg the rest of your life. Go to bed with him as often as you want if you're so crazy about him. But don't marry him—I'm warning you. And for christssake don't let him knock you up, because then you're finished."

I was speechless. This wasn't like Bente.

"You probably think I'm getting mixed up in something that's none of my business," she said, a little more calmly and with reddened cheeks. "But I can't look on quietly while you throw yourself away like this, without saying something. You who—who . . ."

She paused and asked, "Are you mad at me, Edle?"

"No, of course not," I said.

And I wasn't at all angry. I was flattered. Really flattered—at Bente's consideration and at her thinking that Hans Jørgen would want me!

I didn't see much of Bente the last week she lived with me. Mornings we spent on our own as usual and after dinner I went on walks with Hans Jørgen or to his place where we sat and talked. Oh, those long light evenings ... There was a special fragile mood around twilight ... like old glass. It was like a net of fine threads. While I sat there like a spider in wait, thinking only of capturing that poor, innocent fly. I, the dry, prosaic historian, sat there mooning over Verlaine and Maeterlinck, talking of longing, melancholy—the miraculous essence of things. No wonder I drew away from Bente.

In many ways, of course, we were together just as much as before; we went to the University every morning, met at lunch, ate dinner in the city with Gro and came home afterwards. We chatted about casual, everyday things, like a familiar old married couple. We lived in the same room. But in reality we were miles from each other. She was going back to Lillevik, to her husband and child, to her old life, where there was no place for me. And I was letting her go without bitterness. I'd already let go. The distance between us grew steadily greater. Soon she'd be only a speck on the horizon, a name to write to. Yes, because in fact it was I who sailed away from Bente. I understand that now.

Our exchange of letters dried up quickly. She wrote a thank you letter to me, shortly after she'd gone home, and I answered. Afterwards there was only a letter now and then; and during the war that stopped too. Bente hated letter-writing and I can only write briefly and boringly, never having anything to tell. It's been ages now since I last heard from her. She's probably completely forgotten my existence, and no wonder. I haven't exactly distinguished myself in the last years. But I should sit down one day and write to her perhaps. Congratulate her on her honors. Tell her how proud and happy I am on her behalf. I could do that. Then perhaps I'd get a reply. . . .

Did she ever love Sven? That's something I've often pondered. I never really caught on to their relationship. I remember how the question burned my tongue during the last period she lived with me—after Sven had been here. It was the single thing that interested me, and I ached to ask her, but never managed—not until that last day, when there was only an hour until the train left, and Bente was down on her knees, in the midst of closing her suitcase. Then it slipped out,

"Do you love Sven, Bente?"

She got up slowly, brushing off her skirt.

"I was madly in love with him once, if that's what you mean, that spring when I first met him. But that passed pretty quickly. As a rule it does, I guess . . . But yes, I love him," she said, a little impatiently. "At least, there's no one else, as they say. Has never been anyone. It's just that . . . Dammit anyway, there are other things in life, aren't there? Men don't sit there holding their wives by the hand every day of their life. They have their work to occupy them. And home is really just a backdrop, something to come to, a place to rest. All that stuff about always staying home, puttering around being a wife, that's just like having Sunday every day. Disgusting, don't you think? Sure I could do without a maid and clean my house myself. Then I'd have enough to do, wouldn't I? But I hate housework, it's the worst thing I can imagine. I'd much rather do something outdoors. But I haven't learned anything. I can't bear the thought of being put on a shelf, being Mrs. Sven Arnesen for the rest of my life. Would *you* like it?"

My face turned scarlet and I cursed myself. Bente looked quickly out the window, deep in thought, her forehead wrinkled; then, with a toss of her head, she threw out, "But it's a job that needs someone to do it, like everything else. You just have to make the best of it."

Strange that Bente, the childish young girl who escaped from everything like a bolting filly, should have that old-fashioned sense of duty in her. It must be a trait inherited from her father, the medical director, that sporadically asserted itself. Bente possessed it anyway, when it came to "duties"; she always had to see life as something to be mastered and conquered.

I went with her to the train but, as sincere as the parting between us was, there was also something pale and second-hand about it, as if the real parting had happened long ago and this was merely a faded reproduction.

X

Easter came and went. A peaceful happy week. The University was closed, the library empty. Hans Jørgen went with his family to their cabin in the mountains. The streets were abandoned and still.

But Gro stayed in the city. She had neither the time nor the money to take a vacation in the middle of the semester, she said. Anyway, it was a gift from heaven, this Easter week; you could really get something done in peace and quiet, without so many distractions.

Gro's energy was contagious. I settled down at the University library and read at home on the holiday weekend. Began early, just after breakfast and continued until dinner; then I was back at it again. I started to feel I was getting a new grip on my subject. There *had* been a lot of distractions lately, what with Bente and Hans Jørgen and all the lectures that kept punctuating the mornings so you never got time to immerse yourself in anything.

I didn't actually see that much of Gro. She worked until seven or eight every evening, aside from a couple of days when she took off and went for long ski trips. She asked if I wanted to come with her. But I'm clumsy on skis and didn't dare think of the crowds up on the stonehard ski trails of Nordmarka. Besides, I knew she preferred to go alone. But in the evening she used to visit me or I went over to her place. And I felt we got close to each other in those days. We had a special intimacy. We didn't say much; our brains were tired after reading and we relaxed in each other's company. There was no need for discussion or chat. We didn't need to talk; we could be quiet very well together.

I think I've never felt such peace as during that Easter week. It seems to me an idyllic island in a blue, billowing sea—a friendly green oasis where the sun shone. Hans Jørgen was away; Bente gone. I almost think I found her absence restful. It *had* been strenuous being with a person so different from myself, living so close to me on a daily basis. Without realizing it, I'd been living in a chronic state of excitement, had involuntarily stretched up to keep as high as she was. I first noticed it when I finally relaxed. It had been somewhat the same in Hans Jørgen's company. I was always striving to be how I believed he wanted me.

Now I relaxed. For the first time in a long while I was myself. And that was enough. Gro didn't want me to be any different.

I'd forgotten that week, how harmonious and perfect it was. How well I felt. No, not forgotten it, repressed it, pushed it down and shoved it away, on account of what Kit said. That destroyed everything.

I distinctly remember the first day the University started after the holidays. I felt so fresh and alive, my senses new and stinging, as if after a cold bath. Kit appeared, gypsy brown and peeling after "the world's best Easter" in a big hotel in the mountains; she put her arm through mine and proceeded to tell me all about her trip.

I hardly heard anything. Kit had suddenly become so irrelevant to me. I didn't envy her. She was very welcome to her hotel and her carnival and her slalom prize. I had my own life and was pleased with it. I didn't want to change.

"We've had a wonderful time in the city," I said. "Gro and I."

And Kit—I feel ill when I think of it—looked sideways at me, with raised eyebrows and laughed, that dry little laugh. "I don't doubt it," she said. "You two turtledoves."

She laughed again, a little nastily.

"What do you mean?" I asked. My face felt hot. I still didn't understand, didn't want to understand.

"Darling, don't you see?" said Kit. "No, I guess not. Frankly speaking, Edle, isn't your friend a little—well, that way, you know. . . ."

She smiled. I can see that smile, that awful smile. Patronizing, knowing, repulsive. It was repulsive.

I stood there stockstill. "What do you mean?" I repeated. "You're crazy. How dare you?"

My lips were dry. I could barely form the words.

"Oh, I was just wondering," said Kit lightly. "You seem a bit suspicious, both of you. Well, I've got to run now. See you."

I can't describe how that felt. It destroyed everything. It was like a stain on everything I held dear—and it spread, it kept spreading.

Of course I should have talked with Gro, I see that now. That was the only right thing to do. Most likely she would have laughed it away, maybe lectured Kit and given her a real talking to. Gro wasn't so afraid of speaking up. And everything would have been all right.

But I didn't dare. I didn't have a clear conscience. I was afraid. Afraid that Gro would come to discover something nasty that had been there the whole time and would feel disgusted with me. I saw the smile disappear from her eyes, saw her mouth twist in antipathy. Gro, who cultivated all that was healthy and natural—she'd brush me off, the way you brush off a creeping, crawling thing.

I wasn't sure of myself and my feelings. Perhaps what Kit thought was true. Sometimes I almost believed it. And, in panic, shoved it away, pushed it down, where it lay in my subconscious and poisoned everything. Things could never again be like those evenings during Easter week.

Now that Bente was gone, the road lay open for Kit. She'd been afraid of Bente and had stayed in the background as long as she was around. Now Kit appeared. Now she was no longer afraid. She knew from the past that she could do as she pleased with me.

I can't fathom why I didn't reject her, say straight out that I didn't want anything to do with her. Especially after she'd hurt me so badly. I had the complete right to break all ties with her.

But the next time we met, she pretended nothing had happened; she acted unusually humble, flattered me, did all she could to charm me. So I couldn't bring myself to say anything. And deep inside I was afraid. Deathly afraid—of her revenging herself. She was ruthless, Kit, wouldn't shrink from wounding and destroying. She could decide to say it out loud, shout it in the square for everyone to hear, the horrible thing she'd hinted at.

I don't understand it now. Could I really have been so afraid? It was totally backwards. How could *she* wound me? She was nothing at the University, a complete zero, while I had seniority and a reputation. Not to speak of Gro, who was known and liked by everyone. My common sense probably even told me at the time that I could take Kit's sarcasm with perfect calm. I hadn't done anything wrong, and if Kit went around with stupid insinuations, so much the worse for her. But despair gnawed at me; I had a deep, unshakeable belief in Kit's evil powers, in her ability to make things ridiculous, to ruin them, to pillory me, if she only wanted to.

Of course I know now it was sick to think that way. Kit is no witch with supernatural powers, but just a normal person. She's not evil either, as I've wanted to believe, only a little spiteful and thoughtless. She didn't mean it so hastily; she may have wanted to ruin things, but not so much, not to the point that she really succeeded. If she'd suspected the effect she had, she might even have held herself back. She was like an itchy-fingered child, who can't help picking things into pieces.

It reminds me of a fairy tale I read as a child, the Swedish fairy tale of little Herr Pilkulell who had a dried-up heart and everything he touched became as small and gray as he was. For that reason he went around touching everything with his tiny dry fingers—trees, people, animals—and everything he put his fingers on immediately shriveled up and withered, becoming small and gray . . . That's how Kit was. She had a particular talent for putting her fingers on others' joys and making them wither.

She was at the University almost every day after Easter; she "popped in" and fetched me from the reading room; she sat down next to me and Gro at lunch. I fought for a long time to keep her away from Hans Jørgen. But eventually I had to introduce him, and then it was only a matter of time until she devoured him.

Every time Kit was with me and Gro I expected her to allude to what she'd said to me. I was on pins and needles; my palms sweated. Now it's coming, I thought, and hunched over as if to receive a blow—now, now . . . But nothing ever came. In Gro's presence she was always very well-behaved and modest—poor little Kit who felt so alone at the University. But every so often she stuck a pin in me, making a tiny little scratch, so slight only I noticed it.

She began to call me "Professor Henriksen." It was supposed to be a joke, but I didn't like it. Odd—Bente and Gro had also joked about it: "Imagine the day when we'll go hear Edle Henriksen." But this was done quite differently.

"Would you please stop calling me this stupid name," I burst out one day.

"But darling, it's just a joke," said Kit and was virtuously indignant; I was just a stick in the mud who couldn't understand a joke.

"Isn't it, Gro?" she asked and smiled roguishly. (Gro was there. Kit never called me Professor Henriksen when we were alone.)

But Gro didn't smile.

"I can't see there's any joke," she said evenly. "After all, everyone realizes Edle will go far here at the University. If it had been *you*, on the other hand," she smiled at Kit, "then it would be a joke. Quite an incredible idea."

"Oooh, you learned women." Kit rolled her eyes and shrugged. "I'm groveling in the dust. Poor little me won't say another word."

But she was angry with Gro and I saw it.

*   *   *

"I don't like it that Kit is so envious of you," said Gro later. It was the same evening and we were at my studio.

"It's ridiculous," I said. "She's certainly got no reason to envy me, she should know that herself. But she can't stand anyone else having the least little thing she doesn't have."

"Now I think you're underestimating what you have," said Gro.

"Kit gets everything," I said violently. "She gets everything she points at."

"Hmm," said Gro. "That depends on how you do your pointing. Kit Westman may be one of those who only point at what they *can* get."

I thought of Hans Jørgen and was stung with resentment. As yet she'd barely said hello to him. But I already knew, I *knew* how it would go. I can't say how, but I knew.

Gro looked at me with a gleam of sunshine in her tilted eyes. "But for you to be envious of Kit—you've got it backwards, I think."

It was then I said it. "Gro, you don't know what it means to be ugly, to be a woman and ugly, truly hideous."

Tears misted my eyes; I couldn't see clearly. There I sat, ugly and disheveled, and I sniffled and cried. Suddenly I felt Gro's arms around me, her cheek next to mine.

"Dear, darling Edle, you mustn't talk like that."

I shook my head violently, wanting to continue, but she put her hand over my mouth. "Hush, hush, don't say anything."

I sat quite still, feeling my agitation ebb away. My weeping quieted and Gro spoke softly and consolingly, as if to an injured child.

"Come on, you mustn't say such nonsense. You have so much. A person can't have everything. Both have the sharpest mind in town and the prettiest face and I don't know what else. You mustn't be so greedy. But if you want something terribly, you'll get it. All of us privileged people get what we want. In one way or another we get exactly what we want. All we need is to want it, to want it as strongly as possible. But you have to want the right thing, want what's best for you and for other people."

"What do you mean about privileged people?" I asked suspiciously, hiccoughing.

"Well, people like us, who are young and healthy and who have the material basis for a normal life, for using our talents."

The material basis! I turned as resentful as if she'd intoned, "Trust in Jesus!" You go to someone, someone who means everything to you and expose your innermost soul and then you're put off with the Bible or Marx! To hear Gro, Gro of all people, preaching like a communist convert, a Sunday school teacher!

I reeled off a few biting sarcasms about Marxist clichés for all life's problems, about leveling and dreariness, and Gro energetically defended her radical ideas. With that we entered into an intense debate on politics and social questions and completely distanced ourselves from my personal problems. Gro was unusually logical and objective; it was a pleasure to discuss things with her. But at the same time it would have been better if we'd kept to the personal. It was too bad we abandoned it.

Strange to think about. There we sat, just the two of us, with the evening to ourselves, and I'd said the words closest to my heart. The dam had been broken. I'd stripped myself naked, had begun to expose my wounds, and Gro wanted to console and help.

What happened then? We started discussing politics. I was the one who felt offended, felt as if I'd been given stones for bread. So I closed myself off and threw away the moment that could have given me so much—in blind obstinacy, with a childishly defiant lack of judgement.

And the moment will never return. *Can* never return. For Gro is no more. . . .

Did you get what you wanted, Gro? You who loved the mountains and the high plateaus and freedom. "All of us privileged people get what we want. All we need is to want it." You in the prison cell, in the concentration camp in Germany, in filth and stench and misery. Was that what you wanted?

You couldn't keep your health, you who could walk mile after mile without tiring, bathing in ice-cold mountain streams, climbing over rock-strewn slopes and precipices; you who always maintained that health was life's greatest gift. Oh, Gro, who would have suspected . . . who would have suspected.

I'm crying now. Tears pour down my cheeks, pour and pour. Me who hasn't cried for many years. The letters run together on the page, vanish in tears. It's as if something has sprung a leak in me. I cry so hard, I can't stop.

»Part Three «

I

It's LATE IN THE EVENING. The green work lamp glows. Outside the streets gleam shiny black. It's begun to rain again. Monotonous dripping autumn rain. It sounds calm and forgiving.

I've been out to the kitchen and made myself something to eat and a cup of tea. They warm me. And I've lain on the sofa, drowsing and thinking. But they've been good thoughts, like a comfortable blanket of snow over black and frozen earth.

There was no need to cry for your sake, Gro. But it did me good.

You got what you wanted. Torture, imprisonment, hunger, bitter humiliation and finally an illness that claimed you bit by bit. You wanted it yourself. I know that now.

You got to feel life body and soul, live it out to the full, this life you loved. Life, that is pain and suffering and death. You blossomed, Gro, I know you blossomed.

I understand it now. You can't shut anything out. You have to open yourself completely and just receive. Let it get close to you, everything that is, and love it.

You blossomed down there among suffering fellow-beings, Gro, blossomed as you never would have in normal life. You threw all your treasures into the bonfire and they blazed and burned with a high, clear flame. They shone and warmed like the sun.

How strange I feel. So relieved, as if the pressure has lifted . . . I had resolved to write down, soberly and honestly, what happened that time with Hans Jørgen, the time that meant catastrophe for me, which I myself found catastrophic—that terrible humiliation that has eaten into me like a cancerous growth. And I've put it off and put it off, because I felt I couldn't stand to relive it. Instead I've written about Bente and Gro and my relationship to them, and about the strange wonder of that spring.

But now something remarkable has happened; what was supposed to be the background, the introduction, has become the essential thing. What remains, the part about Hans Jørgen, has lost its significance, has shrunk to an embarrassing incident I'd rather not recall—like tipping your wine glass over at a dinner party, an unfortunate blunder, but not much more, nothing to brood and fret over.

I've been imagining that I loved Hans Jørgen. How stupid and how dishonest. It was Gro I loved, Gro who meant something to me. But naturally I couldn't admit it. What I felt had to be directed towards a legitimate channel. As if there's nothing but purely sexual love! As if love, whatever guise it takes—love for another person—can ever be shameful and ugly.

I think now I can finally finish. With the old things. So I can go on.

It was Kit, of course. Kit fingering my happiness, Kit with her dry little laugh. *That* wasn't my imagination at least. Kit was real enough. My god, how many times she made me flinch.

I remember one day especially. A radiant May day, a real summer day. The heat came unusually early that year. I was supposed to go to the theater that evening with Hans Jørgen. A play of Pirandello's was on and we'd decided to see it together.

I'd been to the hairdresser that morning and it was lunchtime before I got to the University. There stood Kit and Hans Jørgen in lively conversation on the square.

Yes, I'd brought them together myself. It had been unavoidable. But I *had* told Hans Jørgen my private opinion of her. It wasn't nice to talk behind her back like that, but I couldn't help it. Kit with her stick pins and her false, friendly smile. She didn't deserve any better.

Hans Jørgen had agreed, agreed completely. Self-absorbed, superficial, spoiled—they were his words, not mine, even though I naturally joined in. All the same he couldn't help laughing with her and teasing her and—flirting with her. Perhaps Kit worked a little harder because she saw he was inclined to be critical. Of course, what made her most determined was that he was my "friend." She flirted coquettishly and displayed all her charm. Other people seemed dull and boring next to her.

It hurt me when I saw them standing there together in the square, so lively, so absorbed in each other. I ached inside, even though I'd known all along that she would take him. But it was painful to watch, all the same.

I had on my new red suit and a large red hat. My hair was newly done. I felt relatively self-confident as I cut across the square. Kit stood there bareheaded, in a short-sleeved white blouse without a trace of powder on her brown face; her nose was even a little shiny. In spite of everything, I was the one who was going to the theater with him.

Then Kit saw me.

"Edle, is that you!" she shrieked in mock horror, and put a hand before her eyes. "God, how you frightened me! I thought you were a fire engine!" Loudly, so that everyone in the vicinity turned; a couple of medical students began to guffaw.

Hans Jørgen laughed, a little condescendingly, and said that joke was so old it had moss growing on it. But I couldn't laugh. I suddenly felt how ridiculously rigged out I was in my red suit, like an old parrot, next to Kit, who stood there brown and pretty in her simple blouse. My face turned dark red, tears came to my eyes. I felt like everyone was looking at me. That the whole square was resounding with laughter. And I wished that I could die, could disappear.

Hans Jørgen looked at me, almost open-mouthed. It wasn't anything to take to heart, surely? I can't understand now, my taking it that way, but at the time it felt horrible. I also remember that Hans Jørgen tried to smooth things over. He started to talk about the play we were going to see that evening and in such a way that Kit was rather excluded. He must have felt I was upset, even though he didn't get what had actually happened. At any rate, he did his best.

But it didn't help. I was suffering and I couldn't forget it. That was the reason I was so impossible that evening. Instead of being extra sweet and pleasant and really making use of that evening at the theater, alone with Hans Jørgen, I sat upon my injured throne. All Hans Jørgen's small kindnesses came to grief against my icy-cold sense of having been wronged.

It wasn't the one remark about the fire engine. It was Kit in her entirety, the way she elbowed forth and trampled on me. I felt I'd been hurt so badly that I had to have reparation in one drastic form or another. Either a marriage proposal from Hans Jørgen or Kit's head on a platter. He was supposed to say that he preferred me, at least. Completely of his own volition he was supposed to say it, as well as that he disassociated himself from Kit. If I didn't get that satisfaction he could forget it. I wouldn't hang around on the outskirts of his life any longer. I wanted my place in the sun and right away.

In one evening I tore down everything I'd built up with the greatest difficulty during the two months I'd known Hans Jørgen. And when the play was over and Hans Jørgen mumbled something about a snack at the Theater Cafe—rather lamely, for he hadn't exactly been getting much encouragement—I answered quite shortly that, thank you, I had a thundering headache and would take a taxi home. He didn't need to accompany me.

With that it was done. I kept away from the University for two days, was absent from important lectures, sat in the library reading assiduously but with little profit. Everything was as before. Only that I had abdicated. In her favor.

Kit was amiability herself, putting her arm in mine, chatting kindly and consolingly, as to an old dog.

You don't need to be so condescending, I thought scornfully. You haven't taken him away from me. I was the one who let him go.

Naturally I regretted it. Bitterly. Couldn't sleep at night, just lay there, going over and over my own stupidity and what I had ruined. At such moments Hans Jørgen grew larger, appearing just as splendid and alluring as I'd been trying to see him. Why, why had I given him up?

During the day I walked between him and Kit, feeling with every word exchanged how much I was an outsider, a fifth wheel. He never spoke again of inviting me to coffee. He never asked Kit either, that I heard. But I had the feeling that they met in the evenings. She probably sat on the blue sofa with her legs tucked under her and listened to Chopin. But it was unlikely he was reading any poetry aloud. Any discussion of Hans Jørgen was over; now it would be just Kit.

And much good may it do you, I thought. You'll never get any help from *her* in your studies. I acted my part brilliantly, for myself and everyone else. Pretended as if nothing had happened. But inside all I felt was emptiness.

I avoided Gro. Had sense enough to feel ashamed of myself. Gro would shake her head when she heard how I'd behaved. She'd never be able to understand how someone could complicate something that was so easy, to wreck it as I'd done.

So I kept away from Gro for as long as possible. Ate dinner an hour earlier and hurried back to the library. Excused myself by saying I had seminar assignments, lectures and god knows what—until I couldn't stand it any longer. For it came to the point when I had to go to her in the end.

II

IT WAS AN EVENING near the end of May, one of those eternally
long spring evenings when the sun never seems to go down
and the streets swim in a soft, melancholy gold. I can remember how the sunlight plagued me. My studio faces west and I
have both afternoon and evening light. What can be sadder
than the evening sun, finding its way in slowly, in broad,
slanted stripes, forcing your thoughts outside to lilacs and
white-blossoming fruit trees?

There I sat at my desk, reading *The Decline and Fall of the
Roman Empire*, while Gibbon's pompous sentences passed
through my brain like shadowy elephants, leaving no foot-
prints. I couldn't bring myself to turn on a lamp either. That
would be ridiculous; the room was bathed in light.

Finally I got up, grabbed my hat and jacket and went off to
Gro's. It was good to get outside and away from Gibbon, even
though I was alone and everyone else in couples.

It had been a hot day and heat still lingered in the narrow
back streets, those shabby-genteel side streets of the city's
west side so reminiscent of careworn *pauvres honteux*. I
thought that if Gro weren't home, I'd take the tram to
Frognerseter and take a walk through the dark cool pine forest, far from the sultry spring of the city streets.

I rang the bell—two short and one long—and waited a
while, almost sorry that I'd come. I was already on my way
down the stairs when the door finally opened. A middle-aged
woman in an apron and slippers shuffled out on the landing

and called for me to come up. Miss Holme *was* home. She must not have heard the doorbell.

I turned unwillingly and went slowly back upstairs. I didn't know what I wanted myself.

"Come in," called Gro's happy voice.

I went in and almost fell over a bulging knapsack that stood just inside the door. Books and clothes lay scattered everywhere and Gro was bending over an open suitcase.

"It's Edle, how nice. So lucky you came!" She crossed the room, flushed and warm, and gave me both hands. "I was thinking of dropping in on you tonight when I'd gotten through the worst of this. But I didn't know if you were even at home. Come and sit down."

She cleared a place on the bed and made me sit down.

"You see, I'm leaving early tomorrow morning. Wait a minute, I'm just going to get some paper to pack my shoes in. I'll be back in a minute and then I'll tell you all about it."

Gro was going away. Gro too. I sat on the bed and let it sink in. Bente had gone. Hans Jørgen I'd lost. And now Gro. Everyone had their own life and somewhere to go. I was the only one left, doomed to trudge around in dismal empty streets.

Gro returned with crumpled brown wrapping paper and a stack of old newspapers. She waded back and forth between piles of books and clothes, straightening and packing and telling me the story. She'd gotten a telegram in the morning; her mother had broken her leg. She had to go home right away. It was too much for her younger sister to handle all alone.

I thought they were a selfish family to expect Gro to just give everything up and go home. They should be able to get help somewhere else. But Gro took it for granted.

"You know I've been thinking of going to Svalbard this summer, so I should help now, when I can."

So empty. I thought of the back streets when the sun disappeared behind the tall apartment houses, turning everything cold and dreary. It was sad, of course, about Gro's mother and too bad for Gro herself, who had to be interrupted in the semester weeks before she'd expected. But it didn't seem to weigh on her. It struck me that perhaps she was glad to be going home to her boyfriend the dentist. She'd only mentioned him once; but then she never talked about her family either. And I could never bring myself to ask. Yes, maybe she was happy, maybe she welcomed the opportunity. *I* was the one to be pitied—the one who was left in the lurch. Inside I was screaming, And what about me? Am I nothing? Just something you throw off, get away from just like that? It was stupid and irrational, but that's how I felt.

Gro noticed, that's clear, for she unhesitatingly let go of what she had in her hands, shoved away the clothes on the bed and sat down with her arm around my waist. She started talking cheerfully and apologetically, the way she had that time when she was going to the party in the black velvet dress, about how unfortunate it was to have to leave in such a rush. She would have liked to stay through the semester. She felt she'd seen far too little of me lately, she said. But then, I'd been so busy with my seminar assignments and she'd been working against time to finish things by summer.

"Well, it was not to be," she said with a smile. And now she'd have to break off her studies until autumn. She probably wouldn't get to see me before then either. But we'd make up for it during the fall semester, wouldn't we? It had been so nice this spring, we'd had such a good time together. Hadn't we, hadn't we both enjoyed ourselves?

But it was just like that ill-fated evening at the theater. It was hard to get an answer out of me; I wouldn't let myself be mollified. Again it struck me that the people who meant everything to me went out of their way to explain as gently as possible that I didn't mean the same to them. That they had no use for me, at least, not much use. I don't know where it came from, but that's how it felt. I sat there stiff and closed off, pulling down the corners of my mouth in a faint smile of derision. Finally Gro fell silent and looked at me, bewildered, questioning.

"Well, I should probably leave now," I said mechanically. But I couldn't quite manage to go yet.

"Oh, don't leave," begged Gro quickly and gripped my hand. "Edle, tell me one thing. How are things between you and Hans Jørgen?"

"Things?" I repeated and pretended not to understand. But it was no use pretending in front of Gro. Everything false and affected fell like a house of cards before her warm open gaze. So she got the whole story. And wasn't that why I'd come? For her to drag it out of me and feel sorry and console me?

Though I wasn't particularly honest. The way I told it, she must have believed Kit had taken him away from me using all sorts of tricks, and that Hans Jørgen had let it happen just like that. I didn't mention the evening at the theater. I couldn't bring myself to, especially now that I'd acted the same way with her. I let her believe that it was the thought of Hans Jørgen that was bothering me, that that was the reason I'd been sitting there so silent and cross.

"It's so shabby," Gro burst out. "So incredibly shabby. I mean Kit," she added quickly. "Men can't deal with situations like that. They're flattered, poor things. And so they let themselves be caught—for a while. Because of course it's just a passing phase. It's only flirting on both sides. Do you really think Kit is serious? Of course not, she wouldn't marry a poor student. Believe me, Edle, Hans Jørgen will come back to you. And then you have to take him back," she said earnestly, "Because you see, Hans Jørgen needs you. He needs someone like you who can be a support to him and help him keep a straight course."

That stung me. So I was good enough to pick up Kit's crumbs then. When she was tired of him I could have another chance and be grateful for it. Be a support to him! Comfort him and help him keep on an even keel? Be a nanny to Hans Jørgen, how absolutely splendid! But when you were ugly, charmless Edle Henriksen, you naturally had to be only too pleased.

Gro must have read my thoughts, for she suddenly became very serious. I can't remember having seen her so serious before—almost severe.

"Edle," she said. "Do you mind if I ask you something else?"

I nodded, feeling suddenly uncertain.

"Do you love Hans Jørgen, Edle?"

I'd asked Bente that, I remembered—the day she left. Do you love him? And Bente had answered—what was it that Bente had answered? "Yes, but . . ." There was a but, I remember that clearly. And that *but* grew and loomed large. Not for the life of me could I answer Gro.

"Because you know, Edle, if you love him, really love him, then you'll get him," said Gro. "Sooner or later you'll get him, because that means you're willing to accept him the way he is, on the terms that life offers. And if you really love him, all you have to do is go to him and say it straight out: Hans Jørgen, I love you. And then you'll get him. No Kit in the world can take him from you. All she has to lure him with is her brashness, while you have the one thing that means something and that makes up for everything else: love!"

I felt I was turning bright red and to protect myself I asked, "Is that how *you* feel?"

"Me?" she asked, astonished.

"Yes, you," I answered aggressively. "You have a friend too, you've told me so yourself."

You're no better! That was what I meant. How could I bring myself to do it, to her, who did everything to help me?

All I hope is that she didn't notice the sting. I don't think she did, for she answered seriously.

"No, I've never felt like that. But I believe, I *hope* someday I'll feel like that."

"For that friend of yours?"

"No, that will never come to anything. It was a childhood romance. And since then it's turned into friendship. We're used to each other and like each other and get along well together, but it doesn't have anything to do with love, of course. In some way, I've known that a long time. But it's hard to hurt someone's feelings, isn't it? I see what you mean and you're completely right. It *is* cowardly not to speak out. And stupid. Maybe the other person feels just the same, and so both of you go around worrying for nothing. But now I've written and put an end to it."

"Put an end to it! Just now!"

I was dumbstruck.

"It was a while ago. That afternoon I was at your place and we had such a heated discussion, remember? I'd just written to him."

She'd just written to him. And she hadn't said a word.

"You didn't mention it," I said slowly.

"You didn't ask," she answered gaily. "But, anyway, now you know. I'm free as a bird. Free to preach to you . . . Completely free."

"Until you meet Mr. Right," I said scornfully. "And tie yourself to him."

"But it's not tying yourself," Gro objected. "No more than when you tie yourself to life, to a profession, a vocation. . . ."

She had written to him that afternoon, had made a decisive break and hadn't said a word to me.

"But if it's not love," said Gro. "Then it becomes a leash, then it becomes a chain that pinches and hampers you. That was why I asked if you loved him. I see it was a prying question, and I'm not at all offended that you aren't answering." She cocked her head and smiled.

"I love him," I mumbled, my face a fiery red. The words were out before I could reconsider, and afterwards it was impossible to take them back. They had to stand there growing into a wall that separated me from Gro forever.

I never saw her again. She went home and then later up to Svalbard with the expedition. She was the only woman along and they said—it said in her obituary anyway, after the Liberation—that she was the best of colleagues: tireless, energetic, always helpful, always gentle, down to earth and incredibly modest. I can see her roaming around in her old gray parka, happy with her rocks.

She didn't come back to the University as she'd promised. She settled down in her little hometown up north to study the varieties of rock there. She wrote to me—long, cheerful letters. I answered with a few dry lines. At the begining I was so shaken and hurt that I couldn't stand contact with anybody. Later I turned bitter when she didn't come back and just stayed on up north.

She didn't come south until the spring of '42. She returned in a prisoner transport and was imprisoned for a year in 19 Møller Street, before being sent on to Germany.

The last time I saw her was that night—and the memory of it had become soiled and muddy. I've done everything to erase it and therefore my leave-taking of Gro has also gotten vague and hazy. All I have is an unclear picture of her, as she stood in the doorway and waved good-bye, large and smiling. She was wearing a yellow and brown gingham checked dress and yellow socks and sneakers. And she waved and called, "Goodbye, good-bye, have a good summer. Take care!" And something about meeting in the autumn.

I went right home. My cheeks burned; I burned inside. My thoughts whirled. Gro was leaving. Gro too. Now I had no one.

"But if you love him, then all you have to do is go to him and say . . . Do you love him, Edle?"

"Yes, I love him," I'd answered, low and indistinctly. And Gro had *looked* at me. For a long time . . . Gro who was truthfulness itself, so transparent, so whole. There was no shadow of guile *there*. But I'd lied to her, lied right to her face. Unless what I'd said perhaps was true.

In this chair Bente had sat and smoked and grappled with her problems. "I love him, but . . ." Wasn't there always a but? At any rate for commonplace people like us? We couldn't all be like Gro. And wasn't it wrong to be so dependent on a girlfriend? Wasn't there something unhealthy about such blind idolatry. I heard Kit snickering, "You two turtledoves," and writhed and moaned in shame.

Oh, I was going to show them—show Kit, show Gro, show them all, that I too. . . .

I drank one cup of glowing black-brown tea after another. My hands were shaking so much that the cup clattered against the saucer. When the clock struck eleven I stripped off my clothes, showered and dressed again carefully; I put on my red suit, powdered my face, added lipstick and perfume, and went to Hans Jørgen's. Went to present myself on a silver platter, to offer myself just like a tart.

Why did I do it? I can't believe it was anything so banal, so ladies' magazine romantic as the notion of "surrendering my-self" that lay behind it. It was more likely the fear of empti-ness, of being left alone in a shadow world when everyone else abandoned me, each for his or her own reality, a desperate urge for action, for once in my life to take my fate in my hands. I wanted out of that shut-off world of books I lived in. I too wanted a place in the real world, wanted something concrete, tangible to cling to—something that was visible to others. I said to myself that I'd had enough of substitutes.

How sad and pitiful that seems now; the whole ridiculous act was *in itself* a substitute, a wretched substitute for the sim-ple postulate that Gro had presented and that I couldn't fulfill.

But I'd worked myself up so much with the strong tea and all the bewildering thoughts whirling around in fear and shame that I had to find a release.

I ran the whole way, reaching the house out of breath and gasping; I barely stopped to catch my breath before I bounded up the steps. My ears felt ready to burst and my lungs pumped like a pair of bellows. But I didn't dare stop, didn't dare think. I rang the bell long and hard. Now it was done. Relief poured through me. I could breathe easier—straighten my hat, stand erect and prepared.

I waited a long time. My scalp prickled; my stomach churned. Waited, waited. But there *had* been a stirring inside there. He was clearly at home, had probably gone to bed. I bit my lip hard—my teeth had suddenly begun to chatter. I put my finger on the button and pressed so hard my nail went white. Oh, those minutes outside, those minutes that lasted forever, when my whole being knotted up, as if in a cramp.

Finally. Padding footsteps. The door was opened a crack and Hans Jørgen peered out, red-faced, his hair every which way. I pushed past him into the apartment, hardly noticing that he was in pajamas and a bathrobe. Nor did I observe any-thing peculiar in his demeanor. I was far to wound up to make any sort of a conventional greeting and instead broke into a stream of hectic explanations. I was so unhappy and dejected. I had to come to him.

"You have to help me, Hans Jørgen. You have to help me!"

I can't remember all I said at the time. But it can't possibly have been as bad as it seemed to me later. It's unlikely that I could have said straight out what I had come for, that I could have begged to be his lover, or that I could have used the sorts of words that have haunted me since—odious, obscene words.

It is undoubtedly my own guilt feelings that have inflamed the event, turning it into the grotesque caricature that has sneered at me for years. When I think about it rationally, it can't possibly have been like that. I wasn't *that* hysterical.

But I must have seemed completely unhinged as I stood there in my red suit, talking and talking in a loud, shaking voice. It was as if I were wound up and had to reel off all my lines before I could stop.

He probably made some vain attempts to silence me. But I was so overwrought that I didn't take any notice. I remember he took me by the arm, gently, as if to hold me back. He probably tried to say something, wanted to explain that now wasn't a suitable time, to invite me back another day instead.

But I didn't want to hear, wouldn't let myself be stopped. He mustn't think I was hysterical, that I didn't know what I was doing. I wanted to show that on my side it was serious. I no longer wanted to be put off with all those words. I wanted something to happen. And so I tore myself way and went right in.

"Edle!" called Hans Jørgen behind me. But it was too late. There I stood in the open door in my red suit, all dressed up, having come to offer myself, and there in bed sat Kit with the quilt pulled up to her chin, staring wide-eyed—just staring. Afterwards I imagined that she had been smiling too—triumphantly, scornfully! In reality I can't have been aware of anything. And for her to smile made no sense, when you think about it. She must have been stiff with fright. Just as terrified as I was. At least. It can't have been especially pleasant to be surprised like that, even if she were the preferred one. When I think about it, it was quite an accomplishment for her to have greeted me and chatted so spontaneously in the street, considering that the last time we'd seen each other, she'd been in Hans Jørgen's bed. She can't possibly have forgotten it. Even Kit would have a hard time forgetting a scene like that.

I didn't see her afterwards. She must have gone to Paris immediately—and probably returned home when the war broke out. But she didn't show up at the University; I suppose she had other things to keep her busy. By 1940 she was already married. I saw it in the newspaper, a wedding in the Frogner church and a reception in the Rococco Room at the Grand Hotel.

Hans Jørgen also disappeared from the University. Perhaps he used that embarrassing episode as an excuse to give up history. He avoided me at least.

Yes, it must have been a little embarrassing for him too. I realize that now. But at the time it felt as if everything were an avalanche, rolling down to completely smash me and me alone. While the others stood around laughing.

To this day I don't know how I got away and out of Hans Jørgen's apartment. I don't remember what I said or did. The corridor is all I remember, the long narrow passage with yellow walls and doors with business cards and brass nameplates on either side. And it still happens that I stumble down that same corridor in my dreams, stumble and sob and stumble on, without making any progress. And the laughter echoes around me endlessly.

Even though I'm quite certain that no one laughed. Not Kit and certainly not Hans Jørgen. But the laughter is there all the same, shrill and biting, irrevocably bound up with that empty yellow corridor. I remember that I lay here on the divan and bit my knuckles and stared out into the darkness with dry burning eyes, and wailed like an animal, while the laughter reverberated around me.

I lay like that the whole night, wincing, my thoughts in turmoil. I don't believe I had a single rational thought. Just lay there and felt humiliation eating its way to the marrow of my bones.

If I'd had more of a sense of humor, that might have helped.

It was comical, after all, what had happened. Ludicrous. The whole episode belonged in a farce. But perhaps that was exactly what hurt worst—that the defeat of my life was *comical*.

It was a long night. As long and as painful to get through as if I'd been struck by a legitimate misfortune—a death, an unhappy love affair. And when I got up the next morning I only had one idea in my head: to forget, to repress.

I hid myself away, like a lobster when it changes shells; I buried myself in books, sat home and read, stayed in the city the whole summer. When the University opened in September I had my armor on. Could go to lectures and sit in the reading room the same as before. But I avoided letting anyone get close to me. The casual acquaintances I'd established together with Bente and Gro withered after a while. And no new ones appeared. I told myself I was armored and secure. Nothing would ever wound me again. But under the shell the inflammation spread and consumed me. Until today.

III

How DIFFERENT EVERYTHING LOOKS when you have the courage to see things as they really are. Now that I've laid myself open, I've become invulnerable. For the first time in my life I'm safe. No one can strike out at me, because I have nothing to hide.

The ugly, festering wound I've carried all these years was healed once the fresh air got to it. In its place another wound has opened, a pure wound of the heart, bleeding like a spring: sorrow for Gro.

That she's gone. Gone forever. How can something like that happen? How can it happen? Someone so warm, so radiant, so full of life! And suddenly, there's only a cold dead shape left.

Her smile, her large, smiling mouth and her eyes with the sunny sparkle. I feel as if they must *be* somewhere—in the clouds, in the sunshine, behind the ridge—they must be somewhere.

If I only knew that she was alive, even if she were far away, in a distant country, and that I wouldn't see her again. Just knowing she was there—that would be something; a consolation, an encouragement—something to live on. Instead of something as inconceivable as life itself disappearing, suddenly, the way a candle is blown out. Inconceivable and yet, irrefutable.

And you have to go on living. Why did it have to be you, Gro—and not me? Why does it always have to be the best people?

Because they're the ones who have courage and generosity. You had everything, Gro, and you gave it so willingly. I had my one talent and I buried it.

You were so rich, you had so much to give. You blossomed and scattered your seeds everywhere. I too received one, a seed I carry inside me. But it hasn't taken root, because the fertile soil wasn't there. Maybe now I can get it to grow.

"If you really love him all you have to do is go and tell him," you said. You believed I loved Hans Jørgen. That I longed for children. "But you must want it with all your heart!" Yes, if I had wanted that I could have had Hans Jørgen. I understand that now. If I'd had love to offer him.

How is it today? Hans Jørgen is still there where I left him—a little further down the side track, a little frayed at the edges, eight years older, more resigned possibly, more worn out. But at bottom the same amiable, incompetent Hans Jørgen. People like him don't alter to any appreciable extent. They don't have the stuff in them for any radical transformation. Yes, I'm sure Hans Jørgen is just the same. I can have him if I want. I too can have a husband and possibly children and be happy. If that is what happiness is. All I have to do is go to him and say. . . .

But can I? Don't the same things apply today as they did eight years ago?

They say that a woman's greatest joy is to become a mother, that love means everything for us women. As a housewife, a mother, you develop most richly. Everything else is just a substitute.

But a man's work is no substitute. A man's job is his life's work. They don't ask if he's married or has children. They say scholars ought to sacrifice themselves to their work, first and foremost. A man can stand alone. He is what he is. While a woman. . . .

They prop up an ideal for us and say: You have to become such and such. They point out a goal that is happiness and say: Go there. And we grow up warped and twisted, trimming our minds, cutting back luxuriant sidegrowths and adjusting ourselves to that one model.

Why can't we be allowed to grow up freely? Why can't a person be allowed to become the person she is and the person she should be? I feel like I've been restrained and squeezed my whole life. Because I was different. And I wasn't allowed to be. But perhaps that's how everyone feels—only I've been too weak, have let myself be held back. Instead of growing freely like Gro. I should have taken my ugliness, my mind, my intellectual ambition, and held them up to the light: Look here, this is how I am! Instead of using my strength to cut them down to size, to erase them.

It's wrong to be ashamed of yourself. Presumptuous and stupid. I've made myself sick with shame, because I could feel so strongly about another woman. I should instead feel ashamed of the years since then, when I felt nothing. What does it matter who you love?

Isn't it the feeling that means something? A child can cry itself sick over a dead bird. And as an adult squeeze out two tears for a dead person. Which sorrow is more genuine? Or more valuable? A shabby office drudge can love his middle-aged wife as passionately as Tristan his Isolde. Is love ridiculous because its object is imperfect and perhaps unaesthetic?

Had I loved Hans Jørgen, really loved him—the way Gro meant—then my love would have been as worthy as that of the fabled Isolde. But I didn't love Hans Jørgen. I loved Gro. And not even that love measured up. Not because its object was a woman, but because my own self stood in the way. I haven't loved *enough*.

I must learn to love. And when love is first there, it will soon find an object—a child, a man or a woman. When you're full of love, you'll find a way to release it. Love grows. And when it has grown large and powerful, it will free itself gently from its object and flow out over the world and the people in it— like sunshine, like warmth, like light . . .

It's so simple. And so indescribably difficult. If you had only lived, Gro. I would have loved you differently—unselfishly, devotedly, putting myself to the side, not thinking of demanding, but only of serving. It's too late now.

My whole life I've hungered for love. Clung to other people, warmed myself at strangers' fires. And it always tormented me that I got so little. All I got was crumbs.

Supposing I started to give now, what then?

WOMEN IN TRANSLATION

Explore the World of International Women's Writing

AN EVERYDAY STORY: NORWEGIAN WOMEN'S FICTION
Edited by Katherine Hanson
0-931188-22-9, $8.95

EARLY SPRING
by Tove Ditlevsen
translated by Tiina Nunnally
0-931188-28-8, $8.95

EGALIA'S DAUGHTERS
by Gerd Brantenberg
translated by Louis Mackay in cooperation with Gerd Brantenberg
0-931188-34-2, $8.95

CORA SANDEL: SELECTED SHORT STORIES
translated by Barbara Wilson
0-931188-30-X, $8.95

TWO WOMEN IN ONE
by Nawal el-Saadawi
translated by Osman Nusairi and Jana Gough
0-931188-40-7, $7.95

TO LIVE AND TO WRITE
Selections by Japanese Women Writers, 1913-1938
edited by Yukiko Tanaka
0-931188-43-1, $9.95

STUDY IN LILAC
by Maria-Antonia Oliver
translated by Kathleen McNerney
0-931188-52-0, $8.95

THE HOUSE WITH THE BLIND GLASS WINDOWS
by Herbjørg Wassmo
translated by Roseann Lloyd and Allen Simpson
0-931188-50-4, $8.95

The translation series is printed on acid-free paper and also available in cloth editions. For further information please write to The Seal Press, 3131 Western Avenue, #410, Seattle, Washington 98121-1028.